CLUB MEPHISTO

BY

ANNABEL JOSEPH

Dedicated to M. le M. with great affection, and to Ghola of the rubber band metaphor.

Many thanks also to J. Marcus for a wealth of fantasies and for inspiring this book.

PUBLISHER'S NOTE

Club Mephisto depicts "total power exchange" relationships that some readers may find objectionable. This work contains acts of sadism, objectification, orgasm denial and speech restriction, caging, anal play and double penetration, BDSM punishment and discipline, M/f, M/m/f, M/m, orgy and group sexual encounters, voyeurism, and limited circumstances of dubious consent.

This work and its contents are for the sole purpose of fantasy and enjoyment, and not meant to advance or typify any of the activities or lifestyles therein. **Please exercise caution in entering into or attempting to imitate any extreme BDSM relationships or activities.**

MOLLY

Molly lay on the cot on a cool vinyl sheet, looking up at the slight, stern-faced woman above her. Ms. Bobo scared her. She felt one freezing cold hand on her thigh and braced herself.

Rrriip.

Owww! Ow! Molly managed not to cry out. She didn't cry out much anymore, not from something so mild as getting her pussy waxed. Ms. Bobo came to her Master's house every two weeks and waxed Molly bare whether she needed it or not. Master was a stickler for personal appearance, and Molly was not permitted to wear clothes, so no part of her appearance could be let go in any way.

Another glob of hot wax was dropped between her legs, spread around perfunctorily by the silent, elderly Asian woman. At one time Molly used to try to converse with her, but she didn't try anymore since Ms. Bobo ignored her soundly and never answered back. Molly thought perhaps Ms. Bobo didn't speak English, but it was much more likely that her Master had instructed Ms. Bobo not to speak to her.

Her Master was the type of man who could get people to do anything he asked. Or demanded. Her Master was a very rich and very intelligent man. That was what drew Molly to him in the first place—his wise eyes and the way he seemed to know exactly what to do in any situation. She had fallen deeply in love with her Master nearly from the start, and she believed he loved her. He'd married her in a very large and ostentatious wedding attended by important Seattle businessmen, congressmen, and people of note. That was their vanilla relationship, the relationship that existed outside the web of daily life they moved in. Their other relationship was more private. Total power exchange. TPE.

Her Master had spoken with her about it before they wed, and she had agreed, *yes, yes.* She loved him. She would do anything to make him happy because he made her the happiest woman on earth. Their wedding portraits hung in a rarely-used sitting room on the second floor, where they often entertained family. It was one of the vanilla rooms. She was not his slave in that room. She stood beside him and greeted visitors and guests in that and a few other rooms which were designated as "strictly vanilla."

She hated those rooms.

Rrriip.

Molly stared up past Ms. Bobo, remembering her wedding day. She had enjoyed the ceremony, as well as the celebration afterward that had gone on all night. But she'd loved the honeymoon most of all, when he had snapped on her eternity collar. It was the type of metal collar that had to be cut off to be removed.

Those photos from the wedding were strange to her. The fancy white dress instead of the nakedness she naturally moved in now. And no collar around her neck, not the slim metal seamless collar or any of the thicker leather collars he sometimes used to restrain her. In the wedding photos they stood side-by-side, a couple. Well, not exactly side-by-side. He was taller and so she was looking up at him, at his thick, wavy blond hair and golden skin. She was the pale, dark-haired girl beside him, fallen into a dream. Even as the photographer had posed them and taken the photos, Molly knew it was false. Playacting. She ought to have been kneeling, naked and collared, at his feet.

Ms. Bobo made a grunting sound and gesture that Molly knew meant to turn over. She got on all fours and spread her legs, arching her back. At one time this had embarrassed her, but now it just meant the bikini wax was nearly over. Ms. Bobo spread her ass cheeks with her gloved hands— quick, businesslike handling. A dab of petroleum jelly on her anus and more hot wax spread between her cheeks. Molly hated the feeling of the hot sticky wax more than the actual pain of the hair removal. That was quickly over, like a massive bandage being ripped off. But when the wax was hot, being spread on her, she knew the pain was still coming, and she hated waiting for pain.

Rrriip. Ouch.

Ms. Bobo packed up her kit and left with the same scowl she'd arrived with. While Molly showered, Ms. Bobo would go out to Master's office where Mrs. Jernigan would pay her and schedule Molly's next appointment. Mrs. Jernigan and Ms. Bobo were equally frownish most days. When Molly saw them together, she would steel herself against laughing at their battle of scowls.

Unlike Ms. Bobo, Mrs. Jernigan spoke to Molly, but it was generally to give directions and relay Master's orders. Mrs. Jernigan was Master's eyes and ears while he was away. She was also his housekeeper and general assistant. There was a chef too, to whom Molly was forbidden to speak, but Molly was never permitted in the kitchen so she couldn't have spoken to him anyway. She didn't even know what he looked like, only that she ate the food he prepared, and that it was very delicious. Well, mostly it was delicious. Sometimes, if Molly was being punished, the chef was asked to make her bland, tasteless things.

"Girl!" Mrs. Jernigan's Irish-inflected voice rose above the noise of the shower. Molly shut off the water and toweled off.

"I'm coming, Mrs. Jernigan!"

Molly was given dinner earlier in the day so that when Master arrived home she could focus all her attention on her service to him. Molly put lotion on her tender, waxed mons, hoping the redness would dissipate before Master arrived and wanted to use her. She was careful not to touch herself in any way Master might find inappropriate. Her sex belonged to him and she was not allowed to touch it on her own. Sometimes it was difficult, because the slightest thoughts of Master could send her slit into overdrive, but there were only a handful of times, mostly in the beginning, that she had been unable to resist the urge to masturbate. Her stolen touches and orgasms had resulted in such agonizing and humiliating whippings she quickly realized the pleasure was simply not worth the pain. But perhaps tonight Master would give her an orgasm...

"Girl!" Mrs. Jernigan yelled again. For a tiny Irish woman, she could really yell loud. Molly took one last look at her naked figure and her shining collar and hurried to the dining room. She stopped just outside the door and stepped on the scale under Mrs. Jernigan's scrutinizing eye, then raised her arms for Mrs. Jernigan to measure her waist and hips with a tape measure. Master required a certain weight, and if she went over it, or her waist or hips exceeded the parameters he set, Molly didn't eat. It was more or less a formality, since Master also controlled how much she ate, what she ate, and how often she exercised. In five years of marriage, Molly had never missed a meal except for behavioral issues. But she enjoyed submitting to the ritual, because it underlined the fact that her body belonged to him.

"Go on, girl." Mrs. Jernigan nodded her into the dining room where Molly found a place set, as usual, for one. She sat and ate slowly, with refinement, the way he preferred, even though he wasn't there to see. She loved being able to follow his many protocols even when he wasn't around, as it made her feel closer to him in his absence. Before Master, she had been so scatterbrained, so reckless. She had lived dangerously and once had almost died. She didn't like to think of those times, and how lost she'd been. She hadn't even realized how much she craved safety and structure until he came into her life.

She'd been working at Club Mephisto when they first met. She still remembered the moment like a movie in her mind. She'd put down a coaster in front of him and looked up to ask what he wanted to drink. His pale blue eyes had fixed on her. Frozen her. He had watched her that night, and she'd begun to preen under his steady regard. How self-centered she'd been back then.

He'd come back again the following night, and this time he'd asked her to go out on a date. The way he'd asked had startled her. "Would you honor me by accompanying me to dinner? I'd like to get to know you better." She had stammered out an immediate agreement, impressed by his handsome looks as much as his impeccable manners. Back then, men didn't treat her with much respect, but then, she probably hadn't deserved it.

But Master had made her feel as if she deserved it. He took her out several times before they began to play. She loved the bondage and his creative approach to sex. Soon he was explaining things to her like protocols and total power exchange dynamics. She hadn't realized how much she wanted strict control and limits until he started to impose them on her. She had curled into his increasingly rigid restrictions like a newborn baby into a blanket. She had felt reborn. She still felt reborn each time his gaze fell on her in desire or approval. When the dinner hour arrived, she knew it would usually only be a couple more hours before he returned home.

When she was nearly finished eating, Mrs. Jernigan burst into the dining room.

"He's coming! Your Master is home early—"

Before Mrs. Jernigan even finished, Molly was flying. She paused just a millisecond to scan her face in the mirror, checking her teeth for broccoli and scrutinizing her lipstick to be sure none had worn off. With a couple token tugs at her long, dark curls, she flew to the foyer and took up her kneeling stance at the entryway just as the lock turned in the door. She bowed her head, kneeling straight, her hands folded in her lap and her thighs slightly parted.

Master is home. Now I can be who I am.

MASTER

As always, she saw only his shoes first, his lovely shiny leather loafers, and the bottom of his crisply tailored and starched pants. She always fought not to look up. She had been trained to let him acknowledge her when and if he wished it. He almost always acknowledged her, but she was trained to wait.

Mrs. Jernigan took his briefcase and coat as always and bustled away with them. He reached down then and placed two gentle fingers on the side of her face. She suppressed the sigh of joy, the shiver that threatened to shake her each time he did this. His fingers trailed lower, beneath her chin, and tilted her face up. She stared at her Master—tall, blond, with blue eyes that sparkled with fondness and challenge. She couldn't suppress an ecstatic grin.

"Lovely girl." He smiled back at her. "Did you miss me?"

"Yes, Master! Oh, I missed you so much. Welcome home."

"How was your day?"

Molly told him an abbreviated version—which books she'd read, when she'd exercised, when she'd rested, when Ms. Bobo had come by. He listened with absorption. These were her moments, the moments he unselfishly gave her each day before he demanded she give herself over to his needs. She basked in his full attention, pouring all the appreciation and excitement she felt into her words, because she knew it would please him.

When she finished, he lifted her to her feet as always and gave her a deep kiss full of promise. She pressed against his broad chest, breathing in his masculine cologne and the fresh scent of his fine clothing. His fingers twisted in her hair, making her entire body tingle. Her naked skin felt alive wherever she touched him even though he was still fully dressed. Only then, after the kiss, was she able to focus again on her task of serving him. She peered up into his blue eyes silently, awaiting his next command, whether it was sending her for a whiskey, or for a whip.

"You seem in high spirits today," he said. "Come into the living room."

She trailed behind him to the adjacent space, a large, airy room with a huge window-wall that afforded spectacular views of the Seattle city skyline. Molly always found the staid lines and neutral tones of the room soothing, and sat there many hours just looking out at the view. But not now. Now she was focused completely on her Master. He sat back in one of the club chairs near the fireplace, beckoning her forward with a casual gesture she knew well. She went to him and knelt between his outstretched legs. She loosed his waistband's button with careful, patient attention, not wanting to jostle or jerk at his clothing. She drew down the zipper and released his hardening member from the fly of his silk boxer shorts. He sank back with a sigh, letting her attend him.

Her Master's cock was truly wonderful, and it was no problem for her to worship and service it for hours on end. It was the perfect length and thickness—it choked her a little when he thrust in her mouth, and it stretched her a little whenever he entered her pussy, but it was a thrilling stretch, not the painful kind. More than that, his cock represented, for her, her Master's awesome power and masculinity. She licked up and down the hard, swollen shaft, teasing the bulbous crown before bowing her head to lick around the base. She caressed his balls as she did, taking him deeper, deeper…

He made soft lust sounds that thrilled her, his hands roving lazily over her hair, down to her shoulders, then down lower to squeeze and pinch her sensitive breasts. She made sounds too, hums and small moans of pleasure she simply couldn't contain.

He was clearly in as high of spirits as she was. It wasn't long before he leaned forward, grasping the sides of her head and taking her mouth in violent strokes that culminated in a pulsing orgasm in her throat. She stayed still, tasting his hot cum, swallowing it down and licking up the very last drops from the tip of his cock.

"Good girl," he said, tilting her chin up with a smile. "Go tell Mrs. Jernigan that I'll take dinner early tonight. We're going to Club Mephisto at ten."

* * * * *

Molly knelt beside him as he ate, in case he should need anything. He was looking over some papers connected to his work. She wasn't sure about the extent of his wealth or what he actually did all day as the owner of a prominent Seattle real estate firm. She just knew he was very successful at what he did. He had a real life name, Clayton, which she also loved, although she couldn't imagine ever calling him Clayton. She had called him Mr. Copeland while they were dating, and Master before they were even officially wed. His friends and family called him Clayton when they came over and Molly dressed in unfamiliar clothing to act as Master's vanilla wife. Some of his friends called him Clayton at the club too.

Club Mephisto. The place they'd met.

Master took Molly to the club on a fairly regular basis, perhaps once a month. Sometimes they didn't go for two or three months if Master was especially busy, and Molly would feel disappointed. It wasn't only that she didn't get out of the house much. To be honest, it was also because of Mephisto himself.

Mephisto was the owner of the eponymously-named private BDSM club Master preferred. Since a couple years ago, Club Mephisto was the only place they went. Mephisto's clientele was hand-selected and thoughtfully chosen. It was Mephisto himself who had invited Molly to work at his club when he'd met her, drunk and wild, dancing atop a table at a mainstream bar on Pike Street. She had shown up nervous and curious, and been put to work behind the bar in the dark, cavernous play space. She had been given a white collar symbolizing Mephisto's protection. What she saw...the scenes, the sex, the power exchange...changed her life.

But she had never been Mephisto's girl. Mephisto was no one's, and no one ever belonged to him. Or perhaps it was more accurate to say that everyone belonged to him in the intimate, decadent world he created. It was Mephisto who had paired up Molly with her Master. He had somehow perceived they were a likely match. It was what he was famous for, and why people always came back. It was why people in the lifestyle all wanted to find a way into Mephisto's private enclave. Mephisto created sex magic, and mind-blowing scenes of power exchange. Molly was not immune to his spell, although she hid her fascination as well as she could. She didn't want Master to stop going because Molly had an inappropriate curiosity about Mephisto. Anyway, *everyone* did, not just her, so Molly tried not to feel too guilty about it.

"Girl? Did you hear me?"

Molly snapped back to attention, flushing red. "Please forgive me, Master. I was...not attending."

He gave her an arch look. "Coffee. And the nipple clamps, if you're having trouble staying focused tonight."

"Yes, Master."

Molly stood and went to let Mrs. Jernigan know that Master was ready for after-dinner coffee, and then went to fetch the nipple clamps from the unobtrusive stash of toys in the living room. It was no less than she deserved. How could she be daydreaming about Mephisto rather than paying attention to Master? Molly knelt before him as she returned, offering her breasts to him as she handed over the clamps. He pulled each nipple hard before he closed the biting teeth down on the tender flesh. Molly tensed at the excruciating pain, but kept her cries of discomfort inside. *You deserve this.* Mrs. Jernigan came in to deliver Master's cappuccino just as he was clamping the second nipple, and Molly's face flamed with humiliation. Mrs. Jernigan soundly ignored her as always.

Master thanked Mrs. Jernigan in a cordial tone, then yanked the silver chain between Molly's breasts.

"Were you daydreaming?" he asked.

He was not truly angry, only slightly annoyed, to her relief. She nodded and answered, "Yes, Master. I'm so sorry and I beg your forgiveness."

"What were you daydreaming about?"

She paused but a second. "Club Mephisto, Master." Well, that was true. She was contemplating the club, in addition to the club's owner. But the words felt dry in her mouth. She knew them for a lie, a dissemblance. She concentrated on the dull, throbbing pain in her nipples. *You deserve this. You deserve worse.*

Master sipped his coffee in silence a few minutes, flicking the chain every so often to draw a gasp of pain from her. She focused all her attention on him, trying to make up for her earlier gaffe. At last he pushed back in his chair, but did not stand.

"I have news for you. I've been called away next week. Business. A last minute thing. I was at ends trying to think what to do with you. It's fine to leave you with Mrs. Jernigan of course, but I think you get restless."

Molly felt devastated, cold-cocked. Going away for a *week?* That was so long to be without him. And it was true. She hated being alone with no interaction or affection, just trapped in Master's home with cold, reserved Mrs. Jernigan. She gazed up at him, letting her sadness show in her eyes. The pain of the clamps, which had given her a place of focus just moments ago, was now overshot by a much more encompassing pain in her heart.

"Now, girl. It's only a week," her Master chided. "You look as if I just killed your puppy. I actually made some calls from the office and hit on a viable arrangement, which is why I came home early."

"An...an arrangement, Master?"

"Yes, I've arranged for someone else, another Master I trust, to watch over you and put you through your paces while I'm gone. That way I know you're occupied and behaving yourself, and you needn't sit around here doing nothing with Mrs. Jernigan. Furthermore, now she can take a short vacation, which is long overdue."

"Oh, Master. You're so smart to think of that." She wanted to ask *"who, who, who?"* but that would have been a terrible breach of decorum, so she waited patiently for him to tell her whom he'd chosen. She knew he would only choose someone very trustworthy and capable, and so she wasn't worried at the idea of being given into someone else's hands, only curious as to whom it might be. It was certainly someone they knew from the club, since they were going there later. The idea of him making the effort to actually arrange such plans for her in his absence touched her deeply.

She gazed up at him. "I love you so much, Master. I appreciate it so much." Her trembling fingers reached out to graze his calf, the wonder of a mortal touching a God. "Master, I can't explain how much your care and concern mean to me." Her voice wobbled on the last word.

"Now there, girl. You know how I feel about you getting overemotional."

"Yes, Master," she whispered, reining in her tears. He reached out to toy with her hair, a light, lazy touch that quieted her.

"At any rate, you may not be so grateful later. Mephisto is an exacting Master. Much more so than I. I coddle you shamelessly."

Mephisto? He was giving her to *Mephisto*? The warm fuzzy feelings of the moment before disappeared as her heart began to race. Her pulse pounded loud in her ears. *Mephisto?* For all her fascination with him, he frightened her. She shivered a little, trying to contain herself. Her Master watched for signs of reaction, and drew her closer when he saw what must have been her obvious signs of distress. He tugged her forward with the chain until she was hunched against him, her cheek resting on his thigh.

"Are you so afraid, pet?" he murmured. "I believe this could be a good experience for you. Something outside your quiet domestic existence with your old, settled Master."

Molly looked up in protest. "Oh, Master! You're not old. Please don't say such a thing! You're terribly handsome and sexy and youthful—"

He chuckled and placed a finger over her lips. "I'm twenty years older than you, which you very well know. Forty-eight isn't so old, but old enough."

She held onto his leg, awash in a jumble of complex feelings. Fear, confusion. Nervousness. Shame that the idea of serving Mephisto excited her, and sadness that her Master would be gone.

"It's only a week," he said again. "I think he could give you a lot of experiences that will help you grow and deepen in your submission."

"You're my Master," she whispered against his knee. "I could never reject any treatment or training you chose for me. If you wish me to go with Mephisto—"

"I do wish it," he said lightly, with an ironic smile. "And you needn't torment yourself with guilt. I know there's attraction between you. I know you desire Mephisto."

"Master..." She shifted in dismay. "I... I..."

"I'm not angry with you. I'm only stating facts. I've seen you steal looks at Mephisto at the club, and I've seen you two interacting. You're only human, as am I. You're a vibrant, sexually alluring woman. I'm not so deluded as to believe I'm the only man on earth who interests you. In fact, if I were, I would be quite alarmed."

She shook her head, unbalanced by the sudden turn in the conversation. Her Master was always blunt with her, but in this case, his words deeply shocked her. Had he truly known her feelings toward Mephisto?

"Master," she said with gravity. "I am yours. I love you so deeply.

With Mephisto—"

She stopped and peered up at him, seeking permission to speak openly. He gave a small nod.

"With Mephisto, it is a...a curiosity only. He's a mystery. That's all it is, the interest I feel. But I could never... I would never..."

"I certainly do not fear you will leave me for Master Mephisto. If anything, I hope your girlish imaginations and daydreams aren't disappointed in the reality of life under his hand."

"He could never live up to you," she said, her eyes wide and emphatic. "My life with you is perfect."

"We do get on, don't we?" he said with tenderness. "I'll miss you while I'm away."

"I'll miss you terribly, Master. Truly, I will."

"It's my hope that Mephisto will keep you too occupied to miss me," he said in a dire tone that awakened a tiny frisson of dread amid all the excitement and confusion she felt. He must have noticed her small shiver.

"Don't fear, girl. I've informed Mephisto of your—and my—limits regarding your person. You won't be harmed beyond the boundaries you're already accustomed to. But I believe Mephisto to be a more...intense type than myself. In more ways than one."

"Oh." She wasn't sure what he meant by that, but she knew without a doubt he would never put her in an unsafe or damaging situation. It was one of the reasons she adored him so much.

Her Master settled her back away from him with a sigh. "At any rate, it will be an adventure for you. While I'll miss you, I actually enjoy expanding your horizons and indulging your fantasies, to a point. I hope to receive you back much refreshed and hopefully improved by the experience."

"I sincerely hope you'll find me improved, Master."

"At the very least, you won't have gone to pieces like the last time I left you for a week."

She blushed. Last time she'd found herself coming apart at the seams by the fourth hour. Something about the predictability and calmness of service fulfilled her. Without her Master's limits and requirements, life became hectic for her. Overwhelming. By now, after five years of serving him, she was a creature bred to control.

Her Master was truly merciful to give her over to Mephisto. It was safekeeping, of sorts. She felt terribly emotional, and terribly eager to show him how grateful she was for his caring ownership of her. She hoped he would allow her to show him how much she appreciated him. She hoped he would take her to bed and let her give him pleasure, but she didn't dare suggest it. She sat quietly at his knee as she'd been trained. She waited to see if he would send her to Mrs. Jernigan for a whiskey. She knew that when he didn't take a drink after dinner, it often meant he intended to bed her.

She tried to make no outward sign of hope or craving—or worse, impatience—but part of her ached to throw herself at his feet and beg him to take her. She loved her Master's cock. She loved his hands on her, his mouth and his teeth and his thick shaft parting her and thrusting inside. Her service to him prevented her giving in to those impulses. She had long ago learned to hold her desires and wants silent like a secret in her heart, and wait to hear what he wanted. She lived to fulfill *his* needs. His collar was the reminder of her status and her purpose. At times like these, when she worked hard to control herself, she focused on the rigid caress of the metal band around her neck and found that submission came easier to her. *I am his*, she thought. *If he wants me, he'll take me. He's my Master, and I'm his slave. I will wait.*

At last, her patience was answered. He drew back from the table, grasped the chain between her breasts, and pulled her behind him to the bedroom.

* * * * *

He was rather tender with her, because he was leaving, she supposed. He pulled her close and caressed her as she undressed him with trembling fingers. *I want...I want...I want...* As hard as she tried, she still couldn't silence her wants and will completely. She had a feeling her Master didn't really wish her to. He took his time, having already climaxed in her mouth just before dinner. He toyed with her, stroking and fondling her in silence as she stood attentive before him in just the posture he liked. He took off her clamps, which he never left on too long for fear of injuring her sensitive tissue. She held her breath and shuddered as the intense rush of blood flooded her nipples. He smiled knowingly at her. She understood that her suffering gave him pleasure, and that this involved no malice or menace on his part. It was simply the type of play that excited him.

He wanted more such play, which Molly expected. He made her bend over the curved oak footboard, and cuffed her hands at the small of her back. He got the whip he favored, a short black implement that hurt terribly, like stripes of fire, and left pretty welts. He held the cuffs hard so she couldn't squirm or escape him. She still often tried to get away, to her shame. Master told her he didn't mind it, that he liked when she tried to evade him, because it showed that she didn't enjoy what he did to her. Molly still wished she could be still and stoic just to show how much she wanted to please him, and how much pain she was willing to take to make him glad. In her heart she was willing to take any pain for her Master. But in reality, the whip made her mind go blank and her body start to panic.

She buried her face in the bedding as the first blow fell, and another and another, hot, aching fire that made a helpless keening rise in her chest. Another blow, even harder. Her legs collapsed and he caught her with a whistling crack inside the thigh as a warning. She straightened her legs again, sobbing and snuffling, offering her ass for more punishment. Again and again the whip fell across her hindquarters. She cried at each fresh blooming of pain, her hands struggling against him where he held the cuffs tight. *No....no...please, Master!*

She thought the words over and over in her head, although she didn't say them out loud. To have done so would have been pointless. She jerked and sobbed as two more strokes fell. Her ass cheeks clenched and she tried in vain to twist away.

And then...reprieve. She lay still, shuddering and tense, her ass cheeks aflame. Master put the whip back in its place on the nightstand and delivered a series of stinging slaps to her welted and punished bottom. She was so relieved he was done with the whip that the blows barely registered. She pressed her hips against the edge of the hard footboard, squeezing her legs together to try to assuage the growing ache in her clit.

Her Master tsked and spanked her again so she yelped and desisted. "Stand up, girl."

She stood and faced him, her face wet with tears. He ran his thumbs across her damp cheeks and gave her an assessing look. "Master Mephisto won't let your hungry little pussy rule him anymore than I do, you know."

She felt ashamed. She had no control over her libido sometimes, a fact that both amused and exasperated her Master.

"I'm...I'm sorry—"

Her voice cut off as he took her chin hard in his hands.

"I am afraid this is another area where I'm entirely too soft on you. You shouldn't be allowed any relief after that brazen display, but I'm quite certain I won't be able to leave you without seeing you coming in that charming way you have. But know this—Mephisto is not so indulgent in this area. I have told him he should not be so with you. Do you understand?"

"Yes, Master."

"This is one area where I'd like to see you learn a little more control. Good slaves should not try to pleasure themselves against the headboard unless Master commands it. Isn't that true?"

"Yes, Master," Molly whispered. "I...I try to control it...it is only that you...I...you..."

"Oh, I understand. It's my fault," he said in a dry, dire tone.

"No, Master! I mean...yes... I mean, the cause of my...lack of control is—"

"My irresistible animal sexuality?"

"Master." She said the only thing she could say without pouring out everything else she was thinking. But he surely heard it in that one word. *Master, take me. Master, fuck me. Please, Master, you must understand how uncontrollably horny you make me feel.*

His lips quirked up at the edges, and she stared at the beloved face, the masterful visage that filled her dreams. The broad cheekbones, the aristocratic nose. The deep blue eyes beneath brows so light blond you could barely see the gray. He bent her over the bed again, still cuffed, still sore from the whip, and positioned his cock at her copiously slick entrance.

"My horny little pet," he said. "Always wet for Master. That pleases me." He grabbed her sore, welted flesh with rough fingers and pulled her back against him. She gasped in breathless anticipation as his cock parted her flesh, entering in a long slow slide that sent electric shocks of pleasure down every nerve. Before he'd even entered her completely, she was shaking in the throes of her release. He didn't stop, only gave a soft chuckle. "So poorly trained, and yet so delicious at the same time."

He continued to fuck her and she gave herself up to the sensations and scents of lovemaking. Her nipples were still tender, dragged across the cotton coverlet of his bed as he thrust into her from behind, so the smooth linens felt like rough sandpaper. She felt the hair of his thighs scraping the sensitive welts of her bottom, and the press of his elegant fingers against her hips and waist. He pulled away, leaving her empty. He swiped some of the copious moisture from her pussy and slid it over her asshole with his thumb. She braced and arched her back, opening for him. His cock hurt as he parted her ass cheeks, but he didn't stop and she didn't even consider fighting him. The head stretched her as it pressed in and she closed her teeth on the coverlet beneath her, trying to endure the sharp ache without making any movements to elude him.

"Oh, Master," she whimpered. He made a soothing noise and leaned down with a hand on either side of her head, sliding inside her all the way to the hilt. There was still pain until he seated himself, and then her body relaxed, finally resigning itself to his invasion. He bumped against her, lifting her toes from the floor as he used her tight asshole for his pleasure. The pain mixed with pleasure at the intimacy of the act, and his mastery over her. The silence of his bedroom was broken only by his gasps and grunts, but then she heard a desperate whine and realized it was coming from her. She twisted her hips, wanting more, and he fucked her harder, grinding against her ass so her pelvis was pressed to the edge of the bed. Then he took her hips in his hands and slowed.

"*Ohhh...*" She loved her Master so much. Every inch of his thick member sliding into her ass was like a gift. He eased in and then out, holding her tight, burying himself inside and then withdrawing. He used his thumbs to spread her cheeks and she knew he was looking at her asshole as he plunged in and out of it. She wanted to look too, to admire the intimate joining, but it wasn't her place. She was glad Ms. Bobo had come that afternoon so her body was slick and free of hair for his pleasure. She wanted to come again and she whined, feeling ashamed, but also wishing for him to understand how much he aroused her.

"What a good girl you are," he said, stroking her sphincter where it stretched tight around his cock. The sensation made drumbeats throb in her belly. Shame, excitement, arousal like liquid fire. "Master loves fucking your asshole. Now I want you to come for me. I want to feel your ring clamping on my dick."

"Yes, Master," she gasped. "I want to come for you."

She clenched around his cock, grinding against the bed, feeling like his fuck toy, his creature. *I want to please you. I love you.* The fullness in her ass and the swirling, building sensation in her engorged clit combined into an overwhelming race to completion. She let go, her arms flailing to be released from their bonds, her whole body bucking with the aftermath of her orgasm. As she came, she heard his groan of satisfaction. He pulled out and shot hot streams of cum over her back and ass cheeks. She lay still as he grasped her hands in one hand and rubbed his cum into her skin with the other. The slow possessiveness of his touch enhanced her feelings of exhausted satisfaction.

"Oh, Master," she whispered. "I love you. Thank you for giving me your cum. It feels so warm against my skin."

"I love you too," he said. "I love marking you this way. I really will miss you." The wistfulness in his voice made her heart start aching again and nearly brought her to tears. But Master had told her not to cry. She wanted to be a good girl for him.

He finally released her arms from their cuffs and then ordered her to dress for the club.

CLUB MEPHISTO

He told Mrs. Jernigan to dress her in the dark blue velvet coat. Molly was happy because it was one of her favorites. It was closely fitted up top, with large tortoiseshell buttons, and flared into a skirt-like silhouette at the bottom. She liked it because the rich blue color reminded her of the beauty of Master's eyes. Plus, it was lined inside with the softest olive floral silk, and felt nice and comfortable against her naked skin. She was never dressed underneath, not when he was taking her to Club Mephisto. The coat came off inside the door to be checked, and Molly accompanied her Master into the play space nude.

She buttoned up until they were in Master's car. There was no luggage to bring for her week-long sojourn at the club, only the coat she wore—which she would give up—and his collar, which she would die to keep fastened around her neck. As he got in the driver's seat and closed the door, she couldn't restrain a shudder. He would be gone for a *week* without her. He touched her knee and smiled sympathetically.

"You'll be kept busy, little one. The time will go fast."

"I hope so, Master."

"Unbutton yourself," he prompted.

Master's sedan had tinted windows, so when Molly traveled in her coat, he enjoyed having her unfasten and open the coat wide for his pleasure. She undid the tortoiseshell buttons and slid a hand down each side of the lapels so the coat revealed all of her front.

"Open your legs."

She complied, and his fingers slid roughly between her pussy lips and then up to pinch each hard nipple. She felt the flood of wetness between her thighs, her body's reaction to the casually possessive way he handled her. She opened her thighs a little wider, wishing she could slide her own hand down there over her freshly waxed lips to the aching nub that probably even now glistened with lust for him. Her ass cheeks still smarted, even cushioned by the silk lining of the jacket. But she wouldn't fidget or shift, and she certainly wouldn't touch what was his. Her hands rested on either side of her, relaxed, slightly open. Whenever they stopped at a light, he would pinch her nipples, sometimes twisting them or even gripping the very edge of the taut peaks so she would have to bite back yelps of pain and mindless begging words. *Ouch. Master! Please, that hurts so much.* And still, the endless growing ache in her pussy made her want to beg for something else altogether.

By the time they pulled up at Club Mephisto, the silk lining of her jacket was soaked with her juices. Her Master made her scoot back and show him the darkened circle as she blushed red. He just shook his head and made a sardonic comment about dry cleaning bills. She melted at his teasing smile and buttoned up before the valet arrived to take the car.

Soon they were inside Mephisto's enclave. A burly doorman welcomed her Master by name, and beckoned over a thin girl with black hair and geisha-style painted lips to take Molly's coat. It was a little chilly where they stood inside the door. She suppressed a shiver as a draft slid up between her thighs to freeze the wet warm sheen still coating her pussy lips. Her Master also handed over his coat, so he wore only his finely tailored shirt and khaki pants. He rarely wore fetish gear—and in Molly's opinion, his business attire was much sexier than leather and latex anyway. She knew other women thought so too, because she saw the way they watched her Master whenever he moved around the club. He was tall, over six feet, and muscular in the natural way of a man and not the showiness of a bouncer or bodybuilder. He moved with a confidence and stride that distinguished him as someone comfortable with power.

And then there was his handsome face, his commanding expressions. It was so effortless with him. He turned to her and she was already falling to her knees before he ordered her to. Sometimes he let her walk, when the club was crowded, but today he wanted her to crawl beside him. Crawling was something she'd had to grow accustomed to, but she could do it now very gracefully and almost seductively. He took out a silver chain leash and hooked it to the ring on her collar, and then led her across the floor. Mephisto's was impeccably clean, and the common areas were carpeted with a deep dark gray shag that felt soft against her hands and knees. She often curled up at Master's feet on that shag carpet as he talked to other patrons or watched scenes in one of the surrounding play areas.

She knew to keep her attention on him, but a cursory glance revealed a few scenes in progress already. A sub surrendering to a hypnotic fire play session; a severe caning; an involved bondage scene in which a slave was being restrained over a padded horse and tormented with various implements. Her Master led her past all the scenes and past the bar to a large table in the corner of the play space. Mephisto's office, more or less, where he met with prospective members and surveyed the goings-on as head dungeon master and owner. He rose from the massive oak table and extended his hand to her Master.

"Clayton. Good evening."

Her Master greeted the club owner effusively and Molly stole one of her usual fascinated glances at him. He was dressed in black—he was always in black. Today he wore a loose black cotton shirt and black jeans, and his thick dark hair was pulled back from his face in long dreadlocks. The effect was not disordered at all, but very striking. He was nearly as tall as her Master, but he was far more muscular. Even so, when he moved it was with a grace and quickness that seemed dangerous, not clumsy. Mephisto's eyes were dark, as black as his clothing. Perhaps they weren't black, but she'd never chanced to look directly at him out of the cowed submission he inspired in her. So she assumed they were black, for it seemed most fitting. His skin was dark bronze, mulatto cappuccino, deliciously set off by piercings in his nose and ears.

His eyes fell on her then and she shivered. He was studying her in a way that unsettled her. But then he smiled and reached to pat her head, a light touch of welcome.

"Ah, your lovely kitten," he said to her Master. "She's looking as sleek and fine as ever."

She couldn't pretend to herself that his words didn't affect her, but hopefully she didn't give too much pleasure away. Mephisto turned and went to the table, gesturing her Master to join him. Molly took her place on the floor at Master's feet, sitting back on her knees and watching for any cues. But he was focused on Mephisto now, so she attended to their conversation.

With the low hum of trance music in the background, the men exchanged pleasantries and her Master told Mephisto a little about his trip and the work that necessitated it. Mephisto ordered drinks for them from the bar, and Master gave her some sips of water from his own glass. After a time, as their conversation moved on to happenings at the club and local lifestyle news, Molly's attention began to drift and her back started to ache from trying to sit up straight. Her Master must have noticed her begin to struggle. He jerked on the leash and she straightened, but then he drew her head down into his lap and began to stroke her hair. She relaxed against his hard thigh, trying not to drool from the smell of him. She sometimes thought that, like a dog, she could sniff her Master out from a roomful of imposters, just from the familiar scent of his skin and his clothes. She drifted in pleasure as his fingers rubbed her nape and trailed up into her scalp, parting her curly hair. *I love you. I love you, Master.*

Then she realized with a start that the conversation had turned to her. Her Master was explaining some of her routines and habits.

"Of course, for this week she is yours. Feel free to handle her as you wish, within the limits we talked about. I just wanted to give you a sense of what she's accustomed to."

"Certainly. That helps me. And just to reiterate, these are the limits we've outlined here." She heard the faint rustling of papers. "No scarring or body modification, no unprotected sex. What about withholding of food and water?"

"I'll leave that to you. I know I can trust you to act responsibly." He reached beneath the table with his other hand, caressing her cheek lightly. "She's my beloved, and my toy. My slave, but also my wife. I can't expect you to treat her exactly as I do. Please enjoy her as you will until I return."

"And...in the event there's an accident with a condom?"

"She's been sterilized. No chance of a pregnancy, and her most recent STD tests are here. Everything should be in order." More rustling paper. Molly felt embarrassed to be discussed so impersonally, but she knew these were the same questions she would want to know the answer to if she were put in charge of someone else's slave for a week.

Molly felt her Master's leg twitch slightly against her head. "If anything were to happen to her—just by chance, you understand—we see Dr. Price up on Woodlawn. He has all her records and he knows her well."

"Don't worry, Clayton. I won't break your toy. I plan to keep her in my rooms most of the time, and even when I bring her out to share, she'll be well-protected. As you know, my private parties are even more exclusive than my Club events. I am very careful about who I allow to use my slaves. Now, if you don't mind, may I address your slave for a moment? On her feet?"

"Certainly." Her Master yanked the collar gently and Molly pushed up off the floor out of obedience more than willingness. She stood beside the table as both men sat looking at her.

"Master Mephisto wishes to speak to you, Molly," her Master said.

Molly. He only called her Molly when they were vanilla, interacting as equals. She wanted to shrink into herself, but her Master pinched her thigh and ordered her to stand up straighter.

"Molly," Mephisto said with a smile. "I promised your Master to take good care of you this week with his permission, but I require consent from one more person."

She bit her lip, blushing. "Yes, Sir."

"Do you agree to act as my slave this week, giving me your complete trust and obedience?"

"Yes, Sir. If it pleases my Master."

Mephisto smiled at the man to his right, and Molly felt her Master's hand touch hers. "Answer for yourself, Molly. Do you consent? Leave me out of it for the moment. He requires *your* permission."

She felt lost. "But Master! I don't want to leave you out of it."

Now Mephisto laughed and clapped her Master on the back. "Enough. That works for me, Clayton. I'm getting the sense that as long as you're willing, she's willing." He sobered and looked back at her. "What a very smitten slave you are. Your Master is fortunate."

She saw a look pass over her Master's face. She was very sensitive to his expressions and she got the feeling he found Mephisto's tone not completely to his liking. A moment later he rattled her leash and she thankfully sank back to her knees. Her Master would be leaving soon. He doubtless had much to do to prepare for his trip, and with her consent granted, there wasn't much left to do but surrender her into Mephisto's care. She pressed her cheek against his knee, huddled against his calf underneath the table. Fears and worries crowded her head. Where was he going? What if his plane crashed? What if there was a car accident?

What if he met another slave he liked more than her?

She bit her tongue to stop herself from pleading with him to stay, or to take her with him. Why did he not just take her along? Because she might be a distraction. Because, perhaps, he needed a break from her sometimes.

The true answer, of course, was that he did as he wished, and it was not her place to demand an explanation. He did not *wish* to take her on his trip. He *wished* her to serve Mephisto in his absence. She existed to fulfill his every wish. Her fingers clutched his calf, but she resigned herself to going with Mephisto willingly. She heard, with great dread, parting words. Final thanks to Mephisto, a rueful joke about how firmly she'd adhered herself to his leg.

"Well then, she's yours," said her Master with a sigh. Not a sad sigh. She could tell his mind was already back on business. He'd made arrangements for her and now he was unencumbered by his slave and ready to go.

She felt her leash passed over and a subtle tug from a new hand. "Bid your Master goodbye, kitten. You'll see him in a week."

"Now, no tears," her Master said as he leaned down to pull her into a hug. She breathed in against his neck, a deep gust of his scent to savor and keep until he was back again. "Your behavior will reflect on me. I want you to make me proud," he whispered against her ear.

"Yes, Master."

He rose and left, not looking behind him, although she watched him go as long as Mephisto would permit her. Eventually he tugged her leash again, a bit harder, and said, "Eyes on me."

She turned to him, not unwillingly, but she knew her sadness and grief still showed in her eyes. She saw a glimmer of sympathy, but not much. Then a resigned smile. "I don't think you'll be worth much tonight. We'll begin tomorrow, after you rest. But first..."

This time he reeled her in on the leash, wrapping it around his hand until she was crouched under the table between his legs. He handed down a condom, and she could not pretend to misunderstand what he wanted from her. He undid his fly as she unwrapped the condom. It was flavored, cherry or strawberry. He was only half-hard, so she fondled and kissed his phallus until it began to grow in her hands. His smell was not her Master's, but it was not unpleasant. His cock was smooth and his balls completely depilated. Once fully hard, Mephisto was thick and heavy between her palms.

In the darkness under the table she fumbled to roll the rubber down over the swollen head. He yanked the chain impatiently but she was not used to handling condoms. She went slowly, taking care to leave space at the tip the way her Master had taught her to do when he was sharing her with others. Thoughts of her Master assailed her again so it felt bittersweet when she took Mephisto in her mouth. How many times had she been curious about having sex with him? About the size and shape of his cock and how it would feel inside her? It filled her mouth and she focused on her task, pleasuring him and fellating him. She did the best she could, impeded by the table top above her. Now and again he'd press on the back of her neck so she was pushed down on his solid length. Once she nearly gagged and choked, and thought she heard a chuckle above her.

A couple times people came by the table and Mephisto conversed with them. Whether they realized his cock was jammed down her throat, she didn't know and didn't really want to contemplate. As his pleasure grew, he seemed to expand to even greater dimensions and she started to feel exhausted. Licking, sucking, deep throating, pulling back to lick and suck his balls, and then back to sucking again. She began to fantasize that he was her absent Master, and she served him with all the passion and desire she felt for him. Mephisto's legs tensed around her and he pushed her head down, down. She tightened her lips and held her breath, opening her throat for him. The familiar warm taste of semen on her tongue was replaced by the cloying berry flavor of the condom. After several seconds, just as lack of air triggered the beginning of panic, he let her pull away.

"Stay," he said to her under the table. He left and she remained to analyze his feelings from the disembodied tone of his voice. Had he been pleased with her oral skills? He returned a moment later and yanked the leash again. She crawled beside him past the table into the back of the club and then into a living area she'd never seen. There was a private kitchen with a dining table, and then two doors opening to other rooms. He led her into the room on the right. It was large, with a massive black iron bed raised high off the ground. She soon realized it was because the entire bottom of the bed was a cage of thick bars. There was another large rectangular cage in the corner. A girl appeared out of nowhere, a beautiful ethnic-looking girl with wildly curly hair and almond-shaped eyes. She began arranging blankets and pillows in the corner cage.

While she did so, Mephisto pulled Molly up and gazed down at her. It did not even cross her mind to dare to look away.

"You're no doubt tired," he said in a deep, rumble-edged voice. "Rest tonight, because tomorrow you'll serve me at my leisure, and probably need to learn a lot of new things."

"Yes, Master. I'll try my best to serve you."

"Yes, you will—or I'll demand you try again and again until you get it right. Perfectly right."

Something in the way he spoke left her with no illusions that he might be patient in training her.

"And for the duration of your stay here, kitten," he continued, "you'll abide by the same rules your Master set regarding touching yourself."

"Yes, Master." She couldn't help blushing a little at his direct stare.

"You won't want to discover what happens if you disobey me in this, girl. Understand?"

"Yes, Master," she said, nodding. "I understand."

"Now Lila will show you to the bathroom, where you will shower, wash your hair, and brush your teeth with the toiletries set aside for you on the counter. You'll leave things clean and orderly when you're finished, and then Lila will put you to bed."

Molly was well aware where her bed would be. On the floor, in the cage.

She crawled in later at Lila's command—washed, brushed, and exhausted—crouching down so as not to bump her head. It was somewhat exciting to be surrounded by those bars, but somewhat scary. Master had never caged her, and most nights even let her sleep beside him in his bed. The cage was much less comfortable than Master's bed, but she could still stretch out almost all the way. She found a comfortable position lying on her side with her legs drawn up slightly. Before she closed her eyes, she looked around the room again. Mephisto had long since left, gone back to mingle with the patrons of his club. Lila had left as well, after locking a padlock fixed to the cage. Once upon a time Molly would have thought about fires, emergencies. About how to get out if she really had to.

She didn't think about things like that much anymore. In a corner of the room, in the near darkness she could see a slow, blue blink. Camera. Someone was watching for emergencies, which was why Lila had left the lights dimmed but not out completely. She knew she would be safe here. Master would not have left her somewhere that wasn't safe. But there was safety and then there was control. She pushed on the door once, twice, just to be certain it wouldn't open. She tugged on the padlock. No, nothing was pretend here. She was caged, well and truly. But she was grateful she hadn't been put to sleep under the bed, with him above her and no way to see him.

Molly's mind started to drift. She touched the welts on her bottom, just a brush of fingers as she settled. It had made her sad to wash off the last residue of Master's cum in the shower. She might have fallen asleep to the scent of it on her hands. But the welts were from his hand, and that soothed her. She cried a little, turning away from the camera so no one would see her—whoever might be watching her now. Soon she fell into a dreamless, heavy sleep. What time Mephisto came to his bed...if he came to his bed...she never did know.

THE FIRST DAY

Molly turned and stretched, reaching in her sleep for Master. Her hands bumped cold metal bars and she jerked awake. She made a small sound of sadness and frustration, and then realized with a start that Mephisto was staring at her from his bed.

If she had to guess, she would say he was only just awakening too. He was leaning up against a pile of snow white pillows. The forbidding black comforter was on the floor in a heap, revealing a dissonant expanse of pristine white sheets. He lay on top of them, his bronze body another striking contrast. She took all of this in as he watched her in silence. She realized—as she continued to stare—that his cock was in his hands, and he was stroking it in slow, lazy movements. He didn't acknowledge her, although as she held his eyes, one corner of his lips turned up in a shadow of a smirk. She looked away at once, embarrassed to be caught staring so boldly. Whenever she stared at Master that way, he reprimanded her to remember her place.

But in avoiding his eyes, her gaze fell inexorably back to his cock. He was hard, his impressive length jutting out from the cradle of his palm. Now, undressed and relaxed, he looked much larger than he looked in his signature black clothes. She wondered why he never walked around naked in the club. But then, the other patrons would probably find that too daunting. It would cause a riot, she thought with her own half-smile.

"Do I amuse you?"

Her mouth fell open. "No...no, Master. I was only thinking...well." She stopped, blushing. God, she had to pee.

"Only thinking what?"

"I was wondering why you don't walk around the club naked when your physique is so...worthy of admiration, Master."

"Are you admiring me?"

Are you flirting with me, she thought warily. She couldn't read him as easily as she could read her Master. Was he angry? Was she about to be punished? Or was she about to be ravished? His expression held no discernable clues.

"Master," she murmured, letting her gaze fall to his fisted cock again, "if only you had awakened me, I might have served you rather than making you wait."

"I wake you when I like, and you serve me when I say so."

Now he was clearly angry. At least, his words were sharp.

"I'm sorry, Master."

"You were talking in your sleep."

"I'm sorr—"

"Stop apologizing. I'm just telling you. I didn't wake you because I was watching you talk in your sleep. It was rather fascinating, actually."

She wanted to ask what she might have said that was so fascinating, but to do so would be pure rudeness. If he wanted her to know, he would have told her. As she came to wakefulness she assumed her subordinate role with greater concentration. Which meant, rather than continuing to stare at him and blabber, she lowered her eyes and waited for instructions. Any instructions. And prayed that he had plans to let her use the restroom soon.

"Did you sleep well last night?" he asked after a moment.

"Yes, Master."

"You cried a little when Lila put you in there."

The mystery of who watched her—solved. "I did cry a little. I was missing my Master."

"I'm your Master for now. Or were you crying for me?" That unfathomable expression again, and that unnerving almost-smile. She didn't make any remark in reply and he didn't seem to expect one. She shifted a little, pressing her legs together. The situation was growing urgent.

"Master...um...I need to use the restroom. Please."

"You will, when I tell you to."

She fell silent, lifting her chin a little. A silly rebellion, but he surely caught it. As attractive and compelling as Mephisto was, she was having trouble transferring her submission over to him so abruptly. He wasn't kind and affectionate like her Master. He was much more...intense.

Well, she would hold it as long as she had to. If worse came to worse she'd pee in the cage, and probably be forced to clean it up. She lay back down and waited. That was a lot of her life's work since she'd become a slave. Wait, watch, and listen. Be useful and attractive. Obey.

She heard him move, and watched him cross the room to her cage, his cock still at half mast. "Go on, then. Quickly," he said. "Take care of things."

She crawled out of the cage and wobbled on slightly cramped legs. He reached to right her and she mumbled thanks as she headed in the direction of the bathroom Lila had shown her last night. She wondered what time it was. She was hungry. For all she knew it was noon. Or six in the morning. There were no windows in Mephisto's bedroom, and the walls were dark concrete which gave it a dungeon-like feel. She took his order of "Take care of things" to include brushing her teeth, washing up discreetly, and combing out her hair. She hurried, not wanting to chance punishment or displeasure from him so soon. Well, no more than she'd already elicited.

When she finally returned to the bedroom he was waiting, staring at her with his powerful arms crossed over his chest. She froze, not knowing whether to kneel or stand. This was horrible. Had some part of her wanted this? She didn't know how to behave, what protocols to follow. Her distress must have shown in her face, because when he called her over, his voice was mildly sympathetic.

"Come here."

She crossed to him, trying to appear as graceful and submissive as possible. When she got near, he reached out and pulled her against him. His skin was so warm against hers, and so soft, for all the hardness of his musculature. His hands roved up her back, squeezing, stroking. He leaned away and cupped her breasts, gently, just for a moment, before squeezing them and slapping them. Not too hard, but she still flinched. The look on his face frightened her. But his eyes...they were not black at all, but a deep, rich brown with flecks of gold in them. He was not the devil, not truly the Mephisto of his name. He was just a man. She tried to relax, going loose in his embrace. He put a hand on her neck and used it to tip her face up.

"I've always found you the most enticing thing, kitten. So beautifully formed. Like a pretty vase. But vases are breakable," he added, seemingly to himself.

She bit her lip. Her heart was pounding in her chest as his fingers wound in her hair. He was going to kiss her...but no. He was only looking at her, looking deep in her eyes, as if for secrets.

"You're afraid," he said.

She blinked, and nodded slowly. "Yes, Master."

"Tell me why."

She thought a moment, phrasing her answer carefully as her Master had taught her. "You're a very strong man. I know to obey you, and I'll try, but there's nothing to protect me from you if...if you were moved to anger."

He thought a moment, tracing a circle on her hip. "Your Master's directives protect you, to a degree. I won't hurt you beyond the limits I promised him last night. And believe me, I'm a man of my word. But will you move me to anger? I suppose you might. I know your Master has trained you just as he wishes you. I know you're a well-trained little slave. But remember something, kitten. I'm not your usual Master. You'll need to learn and abide by my rules this week."

She bowed her head. "Yes, Master."

He was scrutinizing her again, and she shifted under his gaze. His cock poked against her belly and his hands fondled and grasped her ass cheeks. She flinched a little due to the sensitive welts. He slapped her ass sharply.

"Nice marks. Punishment, or Master's pleasure?"

She thought a moment. "Both, I think."

He chuckled. "Not so perfect after all. All right, kitten. I'm going to get to know you a little better. Go kneel on the bed. All fours. Open and hungry, like a bitch in heat."

She turned to obey, his coarse words resonating in her pussy, making it slowly pulse to life. She crawled onto the white sheets as he opened a condom and rolled it on. She opened her legs wide, arching her back. *Open and hungry.* Fear and curiosity mixed with the sensation of him roughly grasping her hips. She felt the head of his cock probing her entrance and then he drove in, a daunting, humbling burn. He fucked her almost mechanically, with one arm braced on the bed beside her. She felt casually used, which always excited her. She could feel her wetness growing, feel him sliding more and more easily into her slickened channel.

"You like this?" he whispered. "Being fucked like a toy? You do, don't you?"

"Yes—Yes, Master," she gasped. Her hips arched back, seeking *more*, more violence, more aggression, but he only continued to fuck her in that controlled, leisurely way.

"I'm just getting a feel for you. And letting you feel me. You're going to feel a lot of me this week," he added with a trace of laughter. "You're nice and tight, aren't you, girl?"

"Yes, Master. I try to stay tight for Master's pleasure."

"Good girl. Speaking of tight..."

He pulled out and pressed the head of his cock against her asshole. She clenched in a panic, self-protectively.

"Your Master told me you've been anally trained," he said, sounding impatient.

"I...I have been, Master."

"You still need lubricant?"

"He uses a little. From my pussy." *And he's not as big as you. And he doesn't make me feel as nervous. I trust him. I don't trust you.*

To her relief he pulled away and a moment later she felt cool lube plunged up into her asshole. Not that it would save her if he was savage, but he'd promised her Master not to hurt her. She willed herself to relax and press back on his thick tool. The lube eased the way and the head popped in. She groaned, aching from the uneasy pain of his entry, but he pressed ahead, holding her hips. She felt split, conquered. Again, he fucked her with a detached and persistent rhythm.

"Mm. Very tight," was his only comment for a while. She braced her knees against the mattress, trying not to collapse, trying not to pull away. She typically enjoyed anal play, and soon, even through the fear and pain, she felt pricks of hot lust begin to spread to her breasts and her clit. She wanted to rub herself, to assuage the shuddering build of pleasure as Mephisto drilled her ass. She collapsed forward onto her shoulders, bucking back against him. Oh, if only he would let her come—

He yanked her back up and grabbed both her nipples between brutal fingers. He squeezed until she cried out, pleading for mercy.

"Don't come," he warned. "A little reminder. If I don't tell you to come, don't dare."

Molly deflated, ashamed and disappointed. But if he didn't want her to come, she wouldn't. She knelt still and open and let him take her ass in an ever-increasing rhythm. She existed to serve him. She would be his vessel. Finally he came with a groan, pounding her ass cheeks with broad hips. He pulled away, leaving her spread and open on the bed as he sauntered to the bathroom. Still she didn't move, didn't rest her trembling arms or close her thighs the way she wished to.

He returned and she felt more probing at her asshole. A toy—a large one.

"Can't let all that lube go to waste." He drove it home and she felt her internal walls adjusting to the broad intrusion. It was either glass or metal, because it didn't give one millimeter. "If we need to lube you up just to take my cock, you could probably benefit from some more training." He slapped her ass. "The correct answer is, 'Yes, Master, thank you for training my asshole.'"

"Yes, Master. Thank you for training my asshole," Molly repeated. Her legs were trembling, and worst of all, her clit still ached for satisfaction.

"Okay," he said, pulling her up off the bed. "Time for breakfast. I'm starved."

* * * * *

He led her to the adjoining kitchen and pointed to a spot beside the sole chair at the table. She was alert for signals that he wished her assistance, but he turned his back on her as he prepared his breakfast. She sat back on her ankles in silence, looking around the modern kitchen with her hands in her lap.

Once at the table, he fed her bits of pancake and omelet from his fingers, and sips of orange juice that never quite quenched her thirst. At the end of the meal he gave her a tumbler of ice water that she drained.

"Want more?" he asked.

Molly considered the fact that he might choose to keep controlling her bathroom breaks, and that a full bladder could result in discomfort for her. She gazed up at him nervously.

He refilled it and handed it down to her. "Drink if you're thirsty. You're going to be put to work today, and dehydration would inconvenience me."

She drank, searching his face for that ghostly faint smile. After that, he had her wash the dishes and tidy the kitchen while he sat in the chair and watched. She moved awkwardly, still aware of the plug deep in her ass and the fading welts on her backside. She was clumsy with the heavy iron cookware, and slow at washing it. She hadn't done dishes since she was single in her own apartment, and then she'd never cooked, but mostly eaten take-out meals and frozen dinners.

"Not much of a housekeeper, are you?" he finally asked.

"I'm sorry, Master."

"What do you actually do for him?"

She paused and turned to him, feeling like one huge cringe. "My Master keeps a housekeeper and chef for tasks like these. I am mainly to serve as...to serve for—"

"For his pleasure. Pleasure slave." He laughed softly. "You have the looks to pull it off. I suppose he doesn't like you ruining that expensive French manicure."

She looked down at her nails. She'd learned to do them herself, to his exacting specifications. Length of nails, color, even the angle of the curves was honed to suit his preference. But if Mephisto wished her to be the spoiled slave in his eyes, she wouldn't make the mistake of contradicting him. She only bowed her head and said, "Yes, Master."

"What do you do all day? He sends you out shopping?"

"I...I am mostly unclothed in his service. But he buys me some things, according to his pleasure. For when we go out."

"How often does he take you out?"

"When it pleases him."

"*For his pleasure. When it pleases him.* You know the lines well. Now answer my question. How often does he take you out?"

Molly thought a moment. "At certain times, like at the holidays, we attend more parties and events than other times. But I would say on average he takes me out three to four times a month. Perhaps four or five times a year, I help entertain guests in our home."

"Vanilla guests?"

"Yes, Master. Work parties and dinners."

"I bet you're amazing at that sort of thing. Hostessing."

"I try to pleas—"

"Please your Master. Yes. Thanks for the recap. Besides pleasing him, what do you do with your time?"

Molly swallowed, reaching back to touch the counter, feeling unbalanced by his persistent questioning. Somehow it seemed easier to take a deep, pounding assfucking than to endure this probing interview. "I... Well, I read."

"What do you read?"

"Erotica. Current events. History books. Whatever Master feels will improve me."

"Do you watch television? Go online?"

"No. Not without his supervision."

"What else do you do, besides read?"

"I exercise. Master has a gym and a pool. Sometimes I help Mrs. Jernigan with housework. But I'm not allowed in the kitchen."

"Why not?"

"I don't know. My Master's rules. He controls what I eat."

He thought about that a long moment. "Controlling can be fun. And you enjoy this control?"

"Oh, yes, Master. I'm so thankful for it."

"What if he grows tired of all the work of controlling you?"

She drew in a soft breath, and swallowed hard. He stared at her, his cruel question lingering in the air between them like some noxious thing.

"You'll grow old, kitten. You won't be attractive to him forever, even if he does manage not to grow bored of you. What will you do then?"

"I don't know, Master." She spoke honestly. She didn't know, and she preferred not to think about it.

"Do you speak to your family?"

"Sometimes. Birthday and holidays. He doesn't keep me from them, but...we're not very close."

"Hmm," he said. She didn't know what to make of that *hmm*, but he asked no more questions so she turned and completed her task, wiping down the counters and hanging the dishtowel carefully over the bar beside the sink. She was just going to turn to him and await more instructions, but then he was behind her, his hand on her back.

"Hold the bar. The one you just hung the towel over," he said when she hesitated.

She reached for the bar with a sense of dread.

"Don't let go." He pushed down on her back a bit, so she was bent over the counter. Then he left and Molly stood, uneasy and nervous, listening for the sound of his return. Perhaps he would make her stand there holding the bar for eight hours, simply to test her. Perhaps he would come back and fuck her again. That would be the best she could hope for. But part of her knew he wasn't coming back to fuck her.

She looked over her shoulder as he re-entered the room a few minutes later, going hot and cold at the sight of the whip in his hand. It was like the one Master used, the one that had raised the welts just yesterday.

"Eyes forward," he said without anger or any other emotion. "Don't let go of the bar."

The whip came slashing down across her ass cheeks. She cried out as a second blow followed, and went up on her tip toes from the spreading, heated pain. "Oh, Master. Please!"

Another stroke, and another. She writhed, trying to evade him as best she could without letting go of the bar she clenched, but he only put his hand on her back and pressed her harder against the counter. Now she was helpless to get away and the strikes kept coming. Stripes of fire across her ass, the tops of her thighs. She cried out at each one, panicked pleas that did nothing to dissuade him. She knew her only task now was to endure what he wanted her to endure. If her pleas for respite and mercy aroused him, she was happy for that, but she derived no pleasure from the capricious blows of the whip.

She began to cry eventually, sagging against the counter and resigning herself to the crippling agony. He caught her with a blow just under the juncture of ass and thighs and she tensed again, trembling from the effort it took not to let go of the bar and run. Hide. Fight him if he came after her. He would defeat her easily and beat her much harder for trying to evade him. "Please! Please..." she sobbed, and then she fell silent. Nothing she could say would make him stop whipping her bottom, not until it pleased him to do so.

Finally, with one last slice across the center of her ass cheeks and the flange of the anal toy, he put the whip down on the counter beside her. She stood still, sniffling and snuffling, too tired to even move away from him.

"Hand me that wooden spoon, kitten."

At his quiet command, Molly looked up at the canister of tools beside her, and burst into tears again. But she did as he asked, and a moment later, the first excruciating smack fell over the already-throbbing welts of the whip. He spanked her hard and fast, and now she screamed in earnest, grasping the towel bar. Just as quickly, the torture was over, and she was reduced to a blubbering mess slumping against the counter.

He lifted her with one firm hand under her arm and turned her to face him. She swiped at tears but he pushed her hand away and rubbed his cheek against hers. The tender gesture and the smoothness of his freshly-shaven skin settled her. She reached out for him and he pulled her closer, nuzzling against her ear.

"I know that hurt you." His voice was a low tickle against her cheek. "I imagine your Master keeps your skin well-marked when you're at home."

"Ye—yes, Master," she stammered through tears.

"Like him, I can't resist marking that lovely ass of yours. Or at least refreshing the marks he left on you. For my pleasure," he added with a touch of irony. "I wasn't punishing you for anything, you know."

"Thank you for explaining that, Master."

"You're most welcome. Although, of course, you are never owed an explanation."

She was finally calming as the urgent pain in her ass and thighs downshifted into a dull, bearable ache.

"And I have enjoyed talking with you, and getting to know you a little better this morning. Although I warn you, very soon you'll be put on speech restriction. So don't get too used to these chats."

Speech restriction. Her Master rarely required her silence, but the idea of Mephisto doing so really scared her. How could she not communicate, especially when he threw her off guard so frequently?

He took her face in his hands and studied her, perhaps in a kind of sympathy. "Don't worry. You'll be okay. Speech restriction is just one more tool to help you give yourself up to me. One more layer of yourself to submit."

"Yes, Master," she murmured against his palm. Again she was fascinated by his eyes, so deep and beautiful. She was even more fascinated by the way he looked at her. He leaned in closer and startled her by brushing a kiss across her lips. Her tiny gasp was swallowed up by a deeper, harder kiss, and then she was roughly pressed against him, held in strong arms, the same arms that had just held her down and hurt her. She made a soft whimpering sound at that thought, and he released her. The moment was tense, and Molly felt terribly confused by the way she wanted him as much as she feared him. She touched her lips, feeling marked by his beauty and power.

"Master...you honor me," she said softly in the silence.

He watched her another long moment, and she wondered if she had said the wrong thing. But then he shook himself from his seeming trance and started to unbutton his jeans. "You arouse me," he answered. A light touch on her shoulder had her falling to her knees. She sat and waited as he rolled on a condom, and then opened her lips as he placed a firm hand on the back of her neck.

* * * * *

She spent the next few hours cleaning Club Mephisto, banishing every speck of dust and polishing every surface. He didn't just watch—he helped too, disinfecting toys and implements while wearing latex gloves. Molly had never thought about how filthy a sex club like Mephisto's might get without careful maintenance.

He fed her once more, sometime just before dinner, she guessed, based on the rumbles in her stomach. Again, she ate kneeling on the floor, fed by his hand. He told her that she'd be put away for the evening, since Saturday night was the club's busiest night, and he wasn't of a mind to keep an eye on her.

By "put away," Molly guessed he meant the cage.

After that, people started to arrive. Mephisto's employees...bouncers and bartenders, some of them people she used to know when she was on Mephisto's payrolls. He leashed her and led her around on her hands and knees as he spoke with his employees. She felt terribly exposed. She was still plugged from their scene that morning. She was no stranger to long-term plugging, but it humiliated her when people made comments about the end of the toy sticking out of her ass. Her cheeks were freshly whipped, sore and no doubt glaringly scarlet. One of the bouncers, one she used to know quite well, commented that he'd love to squeeze them.

"Have at it," Mephisto offered. "In fact, she's been plugged for some time. Why don't you make use of her ass while it's nice and opened?"

So right there, with the employees coming and going, punching time cards and chatting, the bouncer—Josh—knelt behind her on the floor and fucked her after Mephisto removed the anal toy. A small group gathered to watch but Molly just focused on Mephisto's shoes in front of her, and the leash hanging down from his hand. Somehow she felt like this was bearable as long as he didn't leave her here alone.

But he wouldn't leave. He had promised to return her to her Master in good condition, so he would monitor anyone who used her. Fortunately, Josh wasn't rough, and he finished relatively quickly, slapping her ass to dismiss her once he was done.

Without a word, Mephisto led her back to his rooms with instructions to shower and prepare for bed. Later, another silent, lovely girl came to gesture her into the cage and lock the padlock. Alone again in the dark, Molly contemplated her first day as Mephisto's temporary slave. She felt used up, and very tired. Her ass was still sore but at least she was free of the intrusive plug.

As she closed her eyes she could hear faint noise from the club: the low trance music, the repetitive thuds of contact play, and an occasional yelp or scream. She fingered her smooth metal collar, wondering where her Master was and what he was doing. Wondering if he was missing her as much as she was missing him.

THE SECOND DAY

She was shaken awake the following morning, and found herself looking up into dark, intense eyes in the half-light. He was in a businesslike mood, and put her to work cleaning the club again after a light breakfast. This time he went out rather than join her, pointing at the cameras around the club and instructing her not to open the door for anyone. As if she would!

She had plenty to keep her busy, but without him there, time seemed to drag. When he returned, he brought delicious-smelling food from a local Indian eatery that Molly recognized, since it was one of Master's favorites. With a pang she thought of Master, missing him again. Had Mephisto known, and stopped there on purpose to torment her? Mephisto seemed torn between eating and showing her what was in the black boutique bag at his side. Molly recognized that logo too, since it was a fetish shop Master frequently patronized. In the end, he chose to eat the food while it was warm. She knelt at his side, enjoying *naan* and *momos* and spiced rice that he fed her with a fork. When she dropped some, he laughed and pinched her breasts, telling her not to be careless.

She truly enjoyed these moments when he shared food with her. Even though she was at his feet, she felt treasured and cared for. She sat in a very similar fashion beside her Master at his meals, but he rarely shared his food with her. She realized how very differently two Masters might handle and make use of their slaves. She supposed her duty as a slave was to adjust to whatever her Master desired at any given moment. Whoever her Master might be.

"What are you thinking about?"

Her gaze shot to his. Caught dreaming again. Would he send her for nipple clamps to refocus her attention?

"Don't worry, you don't need to tell me. I can guess just from the look on your face. He's a lucky man to have such a devoted slave."

"Master...I am the lucky one, to be able to serve him."

Her words came close to contradicting him, but he let it pass. "Clear these dishes away and then come join me in the play space," he said. "We're going to embark on a little training I warrant you've never experienced before."

He took the black bag with him. Molly cleared away the dishes, the warm feelings from the meal dissipating into stomach-churning panic. Some new form of training? She prayed it wasn't torturous or painful. She wished she could have had more time, but the takeout containers didn't take much time to square away. She steeled herself to obedience and walked out to the club area determined to submit to whatever he subjected her to.

He was standing beside a padded table, almost like the one she laid on during her annual appointment with her Master's private physician. It had stirrups at the bottom and also attachment points extending from each side—which the other table didn't have. He patted it, with that small, hidden smile. Molly crossed to him and lay back on the cool black vinyl.

He began by fastening cuffs to each wrist and attaching her arms—spread wide—to the extending poles on either side. Her ankles came next, fastened to the stirrups with padded straps. He stopped then, pressing her thighs wide open, and slipped two thick fingers into her pussy.

"Wet, are we?" he asked. "Yes, bondage turns me on too."

He undid his pants and sheathed himself, then took hold of her thighs and pressed into her wet slit. She shuddered at the sliding, stretching pleasure of being impaled on his cock. He entered and left her in shallow movements, bumping against her clit and arching over her. His hands were braced on either side of the table near her hips. *She was going to come.* She was going to die from the bondage, the powerlessness. He slid over her g-spot, creating shivery pangs of sensation and a desperate need for release. She gazed up at him, taking in the bunching of his muscles and the hard definition of his abs. He was studying her, his eyes full of some unknown but rigid intent.

"You haven't come since you've been here with me, girl. Have you?"

She shifted slightly, trying to pull herself from the haze of arousal to attend to his question. "I... No... You said—"

"I haven't given permission, and you've obeyed me. So it's been how long for you?"

She licked her lips. "Almost...well...two days. Since the night my Master brought me here."

"And have you wanted to come since you've been here?"

"Oh...God..." Her eyes rolled back in her head as he swiveled his hips and slid the head of his cock across her g-spot again. "Oh, Master, I really want to come right now."

"Don't," he said roughly. He was fucking faster now, driving her toward her peak. *Don't. Don't.* She pushed down the burgeoning impulse to come, to give in and let the rhythms of her orgasm take her. She gritted her teeth, looking around to distract herself, but his cock was demanding attention inside her, warming and filling her. *Don't.* To her relief, he pulled away from her, stripped off his condom, and shot his cum on her belly and breasts. She tried to catch her breath as the impetus to climax slowly ebbed away. She couldn't repress a little whine. She looked up at him guiltily.

He laughed, trailing a finger through his cum, drawing the warm fluid up and around one taut, aching nipple. "Don't worry. It's okay to be frustrated. Edging is frustrating. For you anyway."

She made another soft sound, of protest or complaint, but he ignored it, turning away to pick up a vibrator. She shifted in her bonds as he eyed her. He took his time fiddling with the different settings, making her wait. She knew what edging was. She already knew she didn't like it.

"Please..." she said softly, but he was already spreading her pussy lips with his fingers. He placed the tip against her clit, just a light vibration. She breathed in and out, trying to distract herself, trying not to focus on the growing heat between her legs. He was patient, moving the vibrator up and down across her button until, despite her best efforts, her hips were moving, seeking needed release. "Please..." she whispered again.

"No begging," he said. "I'm doing this for my pleasure. This is not about you. This is about teaching you just how much control I have over you—your happiness and your misery. Do you understand?"

"Yes, Master. But...please—"

"Every time you say please, I'm going to make this even harder on you."

She clamped her mouth shut and closed her eyes, but that was no good, because it only made the arousal grow sharper, a living need between her legs. She bucked against the buzzing tool, knowing it was dangerous, that she might come—

He pulled it away and switched it off. She sobbed softly, swallowing down the pleas that swirled in her mind. She sucked in breath, making fists in the cuffs that held her. *Just...don't. Mind over matter. You can do this, Molly. Do it for his pleasure.*

A moment later, the buzzing sound again. Her inner pep talk transmuted into budding anger. *How could he expect her to endure this?* He was waiting until the arousal became almost—*almost*—bearable, only to bring her back to the brink of insanity again. She could go two days without an orgasm easily. She could go two months, two *years* without an orgasm, but not when she was being teased like this. She glared at him and he stopped in the act of lowering the horrible instrument of her torture.

"You want to scratch my face off, don't you?"

"Master! Pleas—" She bit off the words, but it was too late. He put the vibrator down and went to select some nipple clamps from the wall. She keened in her throat as he flicked each nipple, knowing full well the pain that was coming. She stared at the clover-style clamps in dread and then sobbed aloud as he closed them on each nipple, his face a complete mask in the face of her obvious torture. *Mephisto.* He was a demon personified. She wailed as he parted her pussy lips again. Just the brush of his fingers had her close to coming. If he touched her with that thing—

She tried to shift away, tried to close her thighs, but he only slapped them open. He pressed the vibrator to her clit and a shuddering spark snaked between her pussy and her nipples. She lost. Her body betrayed her and spun into a forbidden orgasm. She was racked by convulsive waves of pleasure she couldn't control. She was vaguely aware of him cursing and putting down the vibrator. She lay limp, suffused with pleasure, but at the same time, she knew she'd disappointed him. Not disappointed him. Disobeyed him. She could see the anger in his face, and hear it in his words when he told her sharply that she'd have to be punished. He uncuffed her ankles and she watched him go to the wall and return with a leather strap. She was still half-floating as he lifted her legs in the air and held her ankles. But then—

Oh God! She screamed and kicked as the thick leather strap whipped full force against the back of her legs. When she caught her breath again, she started crying "No, no, no!"

Whap. The pain was excruciating, a stinging fire that spread from ass to thighs. She scissored her legs, trying to draw them down to protect herself, but he only leaned into them, pinning them back with a broad shoulder. Holding her immobile, he spanked her again and again. All desire and lust fled, replaced by a desperate survival instinct. "Ow, ow! *Ow!*" She squiggled her rear and yanked at the cuffs on her wrists, but he grabbed the chain between the clamps on her breasts and tugged until she capitulated and lay still. Another blow—punishing leather against her tender upper thighs and the sensitive skin just beneath her ass cheeks. She screamed and cried, but he was relentless. Finally he stopped, laying the strap against the steaming fire that was her ass.

"Are you allowed to come without permission?" he asked.

"No, Master," she almost screamed. She would say anything, *anything* to make the punishment stop. He yanked the chain again, causing a brutal pain in her nipples that was not at all erotic.

"Do you deserve to come whenever you wish?"

"No, Master!"

"Who controls your pussy? Who controls your body?"

"You do, Master! Always!" The last word was a gasp. She howled as he laid one more harsh blow across her bottom, and almost kicked him in the head. He released her to go hang up the strap while she lay with her legs flopping limp, crying. He returned and recuffed them.

"Stop that crying or I'll gag you."

She sucked in the sobs heaving in her chest and wished she could wipe the tears and snot running down her face. As soon as she could trust her voice again, she said, "I'm sorry, Master. I'm sorry I displeased you. Thank you for punishing me."

"I hope you learned a lesson."

She hiccoughed and drew in a bracing breath. "I did, Master. Thank you."

He leaned to wipe her face with a handful of tissues, while words of apology and thanks and pleading fell over each other in their rush to leave her mouth. He finally silenced her with a finger on her lips.

"Just show me that you've learned something. I know this might not seem important to you, but it is to me. I want you to *want*. I don't want you to achieve satisfaction. Not yet. Do you understand?"

She gazed at him, at the stern set of his brow and the intensity in his eyes. "Yes, Master. You want me to be frustrated and unsatisfied."

His eyes flickered, and the set of his mouth relaxed. "Yes. That's what I want." She heard the buzz again and a stray tear slid from the corner of her eye. She was miserable because she'd failed him, but even more miserable that the lessons had to continue. She was usually so good at everything, but this...

He lowered the vibrator directly onto her clit, buzzing higher this time. She was so miserable that the arousal didn't come at first. But he was patient, so patient. She squeezed her interior walls, wanting penetration, wanting release, even as her ass cheeks ached from punishment, hot against the cold vinyl beneath.

"Oh, please..." she moaned, and then squeaked as he slapped her face.

"I said no begging. You're not trying at all to obey me," he snapped. "This would all go a lot easier for you if you'd just try. Is this how you serve your Master?"

She sobbed as he left to visit the wall again, and returned with a small vial. He tipped it against his finger and then slid his finger over her clit. *Oh, oh no...* The tingle started immediately, and then reached a steady teasing burn. She bucked on the table, pushed beyond endurance. The bondage, the ache of her nipples, the burning in her clit, the soreness of her thighs and bottom. He grabbed her face in rough hands.

"Listen to me. Focus. Do not come. I don't care how you manage it. I'm going to tease you, and then I'm going to stop. You restrain yourself."

"Yes, Master," she somehow managed to say. She tensed as the vibrations began on her clit. *Don't, don't, don't*, she thought to herself. *Just don't.* He took it off and she sighed, still tingling from the oil he'd applied to her. Twice more she managed to restrain herself despite his assault, and finally, with a nod of approval, he put the buzzing tool away. Tears were still leaking from her eyes, and she was exhausted. He waited a minute or two, and then he ran fingers up the insides of her thighs.

"I enjoyed that very much, although I doubt you did." She was too wrung out to answer, although she attempted a smile. He patted her stomach and then removed the biting clamps. The remaining traces of his cum were mixed with sweat now, and she was so tired, even the aching sting of blood rushing back into her nipples didn't move her to respond. "Rest another minute, and then you can kneel down here and clean up the mess you made of my table."

She swallowed, knowing she'd be cleaning it with her tongue. Soon he uncuffed her arms and legs and helped her kneel on wobbly knees as she lapped at her juices and the more bitter taste of the arousing oil. When that task was done, the vinyl table cleaned to his exacting standards, he took her to shower. He watched her the whole time, cleaning her pussy and clit himself so she couldn't take too long at it. She was glad at least that the oil was gone, washed away by the balm of warm water. But even after the shower, a half hour after the last stimulation, she was still wet and aroused. He pulled her back out to the play space and finally dug in the black bag.

What he produced was a harness. It was wider in the front, with a plate that covered her clit and pussy. It narrowed in the back to a thin strip of leather. Two dildos were affixed to it. Molly gulped, taking in the black, forbidding contraption. She shook her head as he picked up the vial of itching, teasing oil again and dripped a healthy dose onto both dildos. He gave her a look, and uttered four unwelcome words.

"Bend over the table."

She could have fought him. She could have run screaming. God, she wanted to. But what she did was bend over the table so he could work the two thick dildos into her ass and pussy. She pressed her cheek against the vinyl and prayed for fortitude. What had her Master told her? *"I coddle you shamelessly."* She saw now that it was true. Again, almost immediately, the sting transformed to ache and she was kept painfully aware of her filled-but-unused holes. One more cruel stroke of the oil across her clit. *Aagghh…* He paused, pinching it roughly.

"Oh my," he breathed against her ear. "Still so slick, still so swollen. You must feel desperately horny right now. Desperately aroused."

"I do, Master," she replied in a rasping, halting voice. "I want to come so bad."

"But you won't, will you? And now…" He pulled the front of the harness up between her legs, over her aching, tingling mons. "Now you simply won't have the ability. The oil will be enough of an irritant to keep the penetration from feeling pleasurable, and this plate will more or less put your clit out of commission. You'll simply have to suffer for Master's pleasure, won't you?"

"Yes, Master," she replied, although his questions were only rhetorical. She had no choice, as he said. So she suffered, feeling full and yet too empty, her denial and pain decided completely by his hands.

"Now, kitten," he said when she was securely harnessed, "look at me." He tipped her head back with a thumb under her chin. "I see no more reason for you to talk to me, only to obey. You can obey without speaking. So unless I ask you a direct question from now on, I want no words."

"But...please Master, may I ask one more question?"

"One more."

"Must I be completely silent?"

"Silent? No, girl. I said no *words*, not no noise. Feel free to scream, whine, or whimper as needed. I actually quite enjoying hearing you make those sounds."

"Thank you, Mas—" she started to say, until she was silenced by a quelling finger placed on her lips.

THE THIRD DAY

She awakened in the same state she'd fallen asleep in. Pure, elemental arousal, kept at a constant low simmer by the intrusive harness she wore. After dinner the night before, he'd refreshed the oil that tormented her, and then again when he came home right before bed. All that time he'd kept her caged, so she had nothing better to do than think about how badly she wanted to masturbate, and how she was unable to do so. She'd masturbated in her mind a thousand times, but found no respite. She fidgeted in the harness, squeezed her ass and pussy on the dildos in a focused attempt to relieve her need, but she finally realized that, beside the fact that it wasn't possible...her Master didn't *want her to*. If she persisted, then she was willfully trying to disobey Master Mephisto. After that, she just resigned herself to the haunting ache.

Now, in the dim light of morning, she realized she hadn't thought about her Master in hours...since the harness went on. She realized the method behind the madness, and it frightened her. Simply by denying her what she was desperate for—orgasm—he could focus her thoughts completely on her body and her need for him. For his permission. For his release. For his cock. Nothing else had been able to take hold in her mind except her desire for him and how much she wanted to come.

But knowing the purpose behind his treatment of her didn't soothe the throbbing in her pelvis or the longing in her clit. God, what if he oiled her up again this morning? She lay very still behind her confining bars, hoping he wouldn't notice she was awake. She did drift off a little, exhausted from a restless night. When she came to awareness again she heard deep male voices and low laughter. She rubbed her eyes and saw Mephisto stir and roll over on top of his bed partner. His male bed partner. Mephisto pinched the man's nipples hard and he moaned, throwing back a mane of shoulder length platinum blond hair. He was light to Mephisto's dark, and seemingly bottom to Mephisto's top. Mephisto pinched his nipples again and Molly watched in bitter fascination, feeling the twinge and burn in her own hardening peaks. She wished Mephisto was touching her, not that man. She heard hushed orders then. Mephisto's orders. *Suck me.*

The muscular males rearranged, the blond man kneeling submissively beside the bed. Mephisto stretched out his legs on either side of him, his cock standing up like a beacon in the darkness. Molly salivated for him, and her pussy clenched around the dildo inside her as she imagined his cock pushing inside her instead. The man bent over his cock and worshipped Mephisto, licking him avidly, pumping his thick tool in his hands and then taking him all the way into his throat. Mephisto looked down at him like a scornful god, leaning back and letting the man service him.

Molly simply stared. She wasn't shocked, only mesmerized. She'd seen Mephisto kissing and embracing men while she was at the club, and had assumed he was bisexual. She just hadn't imagined this intensity and the dissonance of seeing such a large, powerful man kneeling at his feet.

She must have made some sound, or perhaps he just sensed her gaze on him, because he turned his head and watched her. His lips were slightly parted, his eyes sleepy with pleasure. The man was lapping at his balls now. Mephisto grasped his head and started fucking his face, never taking his eyes off Molly. He came with a groan, and Molly turned away from him, unable to bear the stark intimacy of the moment. Mephisto fell back on the bed and chuckled softly.

"We have an audience."

The blond man turned to her with a curious look. If he expected to find her scandalized or shocked, he was disappointed, because she stared back at him with the same open curiosity.

"Who is she?" he asked Mephisto.

"Someone I'm watching for the week. Slave girl. More of a fuck toy, but it's her Master's tastes."

She kept her face blank at his words, but inside she wanted to rage at him for belittling her service to her Master. *He is your Master for now*, she reminded herself. *Even if you don't like him.* She was glad he had forbidden her to speak, for she didn't want to interact with him any more than she had to. In four more days, her Master would return for her. It couldn't come soon enough.

Eventually he let her out, and to her relief, he didn't put her back into the harness after she'd washed. She knew that probably meant he would fuck her again, but she didn't mind if it would buy her some small freedom from the device. Still, he watched her closely to be sure she didn't touch herself.

They all had breakfast together. The other man sat at the table with Mephisto, and she came to realize they were simply friends, whatever sexual encounters they shared. They followed no particular customs or protocols, but talked instead about business, mutual acquaintances, and upcoming club events. Molly sat silent, choked by Mephisto's gag order, and not even fed very well, since Mephisto was distracted by the other man's conversation.

Molly really had no friends she chatted with regularly. There were some people who knew her by name at the club, but they weren't friends in the sense that they might hang out together, or exchange phone calls.

For the first time in a while she thought about old friends she'd had, even childhood friends. Stacy, her high school friend that had made her laugh until she cried, and Amy, the crazy girl who was always entertaining her with her active love life. Melinda, her sixth grade friend who had always been a firecracker. Celeste, her middle school friend who had given her her first lesbian kiss. Her first *anything* kiss. George, a true friend and the first boy who had kissed her, a real kiss in the back of his car. Where were they now? What had become of the Molly who knew them?

But this had probably been his intention, to remind her of the friends she'd lost in the course of choosing her lifestyle. Of the friends she wouldn't make now that she'd devoted all her service and attention to her Master. But if he thought it would upset her, he was wrong. Master meant more to her than a thousand friends.

Why did she assume everything Mephisto chose to do had some hidden purpose of hurting her, though? More likely, he just felt like meeting with one of his fuck buddies.

She made her mind go blank, and a familiar peace came over her. It was so much easier to serve than to get caught up in her own needs and frustrations. When Mephisto fed her again, she let her lips linger reverently against his fingers. He looked down at her, perhaps surprised or perhaps pleased. Perhaps he had only forgotten she was there.

A short while later he and the friend went out. Before he left, he locked her in the harness—without the dildos—and looped her leash around the foot of his bed. There was no need for locks or restraints. He knew she wouldn't go anywhere simply because it was his order. He didn't say how long they would be gone, or give any directions for her to follow in their absence. Molly knew well enough what her directions were. *Sit and wait. Don't touch yourself. Don't try to come.*

She wished he'd left a book for her at least. He left a cell phone up on the bed, but she knew that was only for an emergency. And an emergency meant a fire or a break-in, not the condition of her unsatisfied clit and pussy. She almost wished he'd left the dildos in, even with the oil tormenting her, because at least she would have had some stimulation.

Then again—perhaps some stimulation would have been worse than no stimulation at all.

Molly settled soon, lying down on the floor to wait. At some point she must have fallen asleep, and she was sore when she woke up from sleeping wrong on her shoulder. She rubbed it, trying to soothe the pain. She must have been having sexy dreams because she wanted to rub herself between the legs too. She looked up with a frown at the camera blinking above her. She wouldn't be able to get at her clit anyway, and she certainly wasn't brave enough to risk loosening the harness. It was possible he never checked the camera footage, but remembering the legs-in-the-air strapping she'd endured yesterday as a punishment, she wasn't willing to take any chances. But perhaps...perhaps he would let her come later.

Then again, his guy friend was with him. It had been hours now since he'd used her, and perhaps he wouldn't use her at all today, preferring his male lover. She pouted, still rubbing her shoulder, and then heard their voices out in the other room. *Finally.*

But they didn't come. She heard noises, impact, groans. They were playing out in the dungeon. The sounds alone were more than enough to arouse her—she was glad she wasn't watching or she'd really be getting turned on. Even so... She parted her knees where she sat, wanting to drag her hungry pussy across the floor. More thuds and guttural groans. A yell that was from the blond man. He was clearly still bottoming. *Oh God.*

Then silence. *Please come fuck me. Please.* Molly decided that orgasm denial was ruining her as a slave. She couldn't think of anything but sex. Normally she was very service oriented, but now... What if Mephisto turned her into a sex-crazed maniac just in time for her to be returned to her Master? What would her Master make of her, seeing her like this? She closed her legs and attempted to sit primly.

In the silence she heard voices again, moving closer. Mephisto came back in the room, pulling his friend behind him. The man's ass and thighs were now beaten a deep red. She wondered if he'd gotten the same type of strapping she'd suffered. Both men's cocks were also reddish-purplish hard, bobbing and jerking in front of them. Mephisto leaned over the bed next to Molly and gave the man a look. In response, Mephisto's lover scrambled to sheathe himself and carefully coat his cock with lube. Still, to this point, neither man had acknowledged her presence. She watched unabashed as the man grabbed Mephisto's hips and eased his cock into her Master's asshole. Mephisto was beautiful dark sensuality as he received him, his hairy thighs and ass cheeks tensing as he groaned. The other man hissed his breath in and seemed to be trying really hard to hold back. Perhaps Mephisto denied his orgasms too?

"Girl!" Mephisto's bark startled her. He was unlooping her leash. "Go get a condom. Now."

She ran to his bureau to get one from the basket there.

"Lay on the bed," he gasped, grabbing it from her. His fingers worked at the buckles of her harness, flinging it away. The man behind him never stopped fucking. Mephisto yanked her by the hips until she was nearly to the edge of the bed, and then slid inside her. When she lifted her legs to wrap around Mephisto's hips, she felt the hands of the man behind her sliding up her thighs. Mephisto pounded her in rhythm to his lover's thrusts, and she lifted her pelvis, enjoying the fullness of his cock. The men grew rougher, more frenzied. The man practically crawled over Mephisto's back and Mephisto, for his part, fucked Molly right across the expansive bed.

"Don't come," he grunted, pinching her nipple. "You. Girl. You don't come."

She hated it but she nodded compliantly. A moment later, Mephisto shuddered, ramming her hard, and the man behind him groaned. They pulled away slowly, gasping, and Molly lay still, miserable and unsatisfied. She didn't watch as Mephisto embraced his lover and kissed him. She wanted to die.

He ignored her the rest of the day, until she was going mad from boredom. She eavesdropped on their conversations, feeling hopelessly banal compared to Mephisto's friend, who she eventually divined was some kind of musical artist on a tour.

Later, just before bed, they fucked her again, this time on the floor in a different arrangement. She was again on her back, her shoulder blades sliding across the floor as the blond man—Jamie—fucked her pussy, and Mephisto fucked him from behind. She found it traumatic, because she had taken a great dislike to Jamie, and she had a suspicion that the feeling was mutual. That suspicion was confirmed as they lay together afterward. Jamie looked at Mephisto, dead serious.

"Didn't you tell me your slave was on orgasm restriction?"

Molly stared at the blond man, confused at first, but then outraged when understanding dawned. Mephisto gazed at her, and she shook her head with all the insistence she could muster. *No, no! I didn't! No!*

"She's good at hiding it," Jamie went on, "but I felt it. I felt it on my cock."

Liar. You're such a liar. Mephisto had to see through him, but damn, he was a really talented liar. Mephisto considered another moment.

Ask me. Ask me, I'll tell you. I didn't. She kept shaking her head, but in her desperation to avoid punishment, she was sure her denial seemed exaggerated and over the top.

Mephisto seemed to make a decision then, and it wasn't in her favor. "Let's take her out to the cross." She drew back, still shaking her head, as if she might finally get through to him. Jamie and Mephisto both pulled her up, carrying her resisting form out into the dungeon's play space. It was so unfair! So sickeningly unfair! If she'd known she'd be punished anyway, she would have gone ahead and had an orgasm. She dug her heels in when they got to the cross, turning to Mephisto, close to tears.

"He's lying!" she finally burst out. "I don't know why, but he's ly—"

His big fingers came over her face, squeezing her mouth shut. "And you're on speech restriction, bad girl. Who gave you permission to speak?"

She started to cry in earnest, the unfairness of the situation pressing down on her already defeated shoulders. She knew it was never about fair or unfair where slavery was concerned. But it smarted to be called a bad girl when she'd been trying so hard to be good, and to not even have enjoyed the orgasm she was about to be punished for. She still fought as they cuffed her hands and feet to the x-shaped cross with her back exposed.

"Get me the snake whip," Mephisto said when they were finished. Molly shook with bitter sobs, pressing her belly to the smooth wood in front of her. *Unfair or not, you are his to use or abuse,* her mind whispered. *You chose this.*

The first lash, a molten flick across her bottom, took her feet out from under her. She hung in her bonds, gasping for breath through tears. "Up," he ordered, delivering another one to the outside of her flank. She struggled, she fought, but she went nowhere. The lash kept falling, on the back of her thighs, her ass, her back and shoulders. Jamie was silent, but no doubt he was enjoying watching her take this punishment he'd caused. With that thought in mind, she tried to steel herself to dignified silence, but that only lasted a few minutes before she gave way to whimpers, and soon enough, screams. She never knew where he would strike her next— and each strike was clearly focused. He wasn't just flailing, but hit her in areas calculated to hurt. The sound of the whip's crack scared her as badly as the searing contact. She started to shake, gritting her teeth to stop from begging for mercy. It had been fifteen minutes at least. Twenty minutes. Half an hour.

Finally he stopped, but only to turn her around and fix her with her front facing out. Still she screamed, jerking in her bonds as he flicked fiery pain on belly, thighs, nipples, breasts. In between screams, she sobbed, and then she fell silent, praying inside her head. She didn't pray to God. She shut her eyes tight and prayed to Master. *Please, please, come and get me. Please, I miss you. I love you. Why did you leave me here?*

"Look at me!"

Her eyes opened, focused and unfocused. Why did he look so angry? Jamie was watching over his shoulder, aroused, fisting his cock. If Jamie tried to fuck her again she'd gouge his eyes out, with her teeth if she had to.

"Look at me," Mephisto barked again.

She stared in his eyes, flinched and moaned as he landed the lash on each breast. She knew what he wanted, although it was a struggle to get there. She disciplined her face to blank acceptance. He wanted her to acknowledge him as her Master, with the right to hurt her if he wanted, without anger or resistance on her part. She relaxed her body and let her arms fall open to him. *I am yours. I am yours.* She repeated it in her mind until she managed to convince both herself and him. Once her eyes communicated that submission he sought, he coiled the whip in his fist. He went to hang it up, returning with a set of clamps.

He wiped her tearful face with rough fingers as she stood unresisting. *I am yours. I am yours. Use me. Hurt me as you will.* Without words he applied a clamp to each nipple, and then drew a center clamp down her belly, down between her legs, where he parted her pussy lips with clinical detachment. He drew back her clitoral hood and clipped the last clamp directly to the throbbing flesh there. From violence and the battle of submission, she was copiously wet. Her breasts seemed to swell and her pussy clenched at the exquisite torture centered on her clit. Again she was climbing to the precipice of arousal. Not a precipice. A plateau, where she would wait and ache and remain unsatisfied.

He left her there perhaps another half hour, retiring to the bedroom with his friend. Finally they came out and Jamie left. It was late. She was hungry and tired, and mentally exhausted from the trial she'd endured. *Still four more days to go.* The thought of it almost destroyed her. But it was really only three days, because this day was nearly over, and her Master would come for her sometime on the last day. *What if he doesn't come though?* some part of her whispered. *What if he is delayed? What if you have to stay another day? Another week?*

That thought brought her to tears again. He stood four or five feet away, just watching her cry.

"It's hard, girl, isn't it?"

The tenderness in his voice hurt almost as much as the lash he'd wielded. He came and removed the clamps, then released her from the cuffs that held her. She didn't want to be touched, but she couldn't stand on her own and so he picked her up and carried her against his chest. He took her to the kitchen and set her on the floor, fixing a dinner in the stultifying silence. Molly was thankful for the speech restriction that had seemed a burden just a couple hours ago. If he had asked her to express her feelings or thoughts, she couldn't have done it. She wanted silence and solitude. She was stuck in a battle of wills between her outraged sense of justice and her desire to be a good slave.

When he sat and offered her food, she took it only with the greatest reluctance. When she almost vomited he didn't give her any more, but he made her drink water, holding the cup to her lips when she would have refused it. After that he soaked her in his tub, in warm, soapy water, carefully inspecting the few whip marks that had broken her skin. Molly knew they would fade by the time her Master returned, leaving no noticeable scars, but he still made her stand while he cleaned and applied antibiotic cream to each cut.

By that point she wished for nothing more than bed. Caged isolation. She crawled in gratefully when he opened the door for her, and was almost asleep by the time she heard the lock slip home. The last thing she thought before she drifted off to sleep was *three more days. Please let me survive three more days.*

THE FOURTH DAY

The dungeon looked different in the light, she thought. She was on Mephisto's lap, her back to his front, being fed lunch at his work table. She was plugged and harnessed again after a welcome night of respite. She couldn't have summoned the energy to masturbate last night anyway. But he was wise to have harnessed her now, because the days of teasing and denial were starting to take a toll on her.

And the teasing never stopped. He'd loosened the harness enough to slide a couple agile fingers down the front. He tormented her every so often, running fleeting touches over her slick clit. He'd use those same fingers to feed her pieces of bread and hummus, so she would taste herself on them, an added seasoning that only reminded her of her frustration. Longing sauce.

She'd slept late, having vivid dreams of Master, and Mephisto had been kind enough not to wake her until she came to wakefulness on her own. She still felt groggy and was thankful that—for the moment anyway—Mephisto was in a relaxed mood. She leaned her head back on his shoulder and he absently toyed with her breasts between swipes at her aching pussy. She felt loose and surrendered, letting his warmth seep into her from the muscles at her back. "Little Miss Molly," he sighed against her ear as he fed her a piece of pineapple. "Aren't you sweet?"

She stiffened a little. Somehow it was unsettling to hear him say her name. But of course he knew her name...she'd worked for him once upon a time, in another life. "Sweet little Molly," he said again, turning her head to lick pineapple juice from her lips, noting the gravity in her expression.

"What is it, girl? Forget your name? It's Molly." He was teasing her. He kissed her again, more deeply this time. He was a passionate, talented kisser, a skill that melted her. Master kissed her often, but his kisses tended to have a paternal, doting quality. Mephisto kissed her like the boys used to kiss her behind the gym in school. As he kissed her, his fingers grazed her clit again and she moaned a feeble protest. He pulled away and she pressed her head into his neck, ashamed to be complaining. He didn't seem angry though. He threaded fingers through her hair, his other hand still pressed against her pussy.

"I know a lot about you, girl. You'd probably be surprised," he went on in a softer voice, almost as though he were confiding in her. "I know your maiden name was Molly Grace Belden, and your married name is Molly Grace Copeland. I know your birthday is April seventh, and that you were born and raised in Bloomington. I know you have an environmental science degree from IU."

Molly tried to block out his words, not wanting to remember her life before Master. Not that she hadn't enjoyed it. It was just...the past. Something she'd given up. No, not given up. That sounded so negative. She'd left all that behind for something better. Master, and Master's happiness. His warmth and the soothing structure of his daily requirements.

"I know something else about you," he said. "I know you didn't really come yesterday."

She wished he hadn't told her. The only thing that had made the unfairness bearable was that she thought he really believed she'd done it.

But all along he'd known Jamie was lying. She hated him suddenly, even his soft voice, his tenderness. She tried not to let it show, hiding her face against his neck. Willing herself to subordination. He nudged her back, gazing down at her.

"You're wondering why I punished you when I knew? I was punishing you for speaking, for protesting. For your tone. And because it pleases me to hurt you sometimes just because I can. Just because I enjoy pushing you to your limits and watching you break down."

His fingers moved again on her clit, splintering her attention with soft, provoking taps. She tried not to move her hips, not to press against him begging for more. He chuckled softly, no doubt feeling the vibration of need she could never really hide.

"It's the same thing with the orgasm denial, kitten. I enjoy watching the build up, seeing how far I can tease and wrap you around my fingers. How much I can make you dance." She pressed harder against his neck, the quiet, pedantic tone of his voice mesmerizing her. Meanwhile, his finger kept stroking her in the same lilting rhythm of his speech. "The denial is just a tool for winding you up so I can watch you writhe and wriggle for me."

Oh...ohhh... Despite her best intentions she moved her hips and whimpered a little. He wouldn't let her get away, but held her closer instead, subjecting her to his tempting ministrations. Her pussy was clenching on the protrusion inside, wanting more stimulation. Even an assfucking...

"You see?" He chuckled softly against her ear. "Not letting you come...it's like the rubber band on those little wooden airplane toys: You twist and twist them until you can't twist them anymore, then you let it go and watch them fly around the room."

Molly frowned, seeing his perspective, but wishing she could verbalize her own. *If you twist too much, Master, the toy will break.* She turned away from the haven of his warm skin, from the curve of his neck. He pulled his hand out of the harness and grasped her face, forcing her gaze back to his.

"You have to trust me, girl. I think you don't trust me. I know we haven't had a lot of time together, but I'm being careful. Perhaps you don't see it, but I am."

She tried to go soft, tried to be pleasing to him. It was a struggle. *This is so hard.* It was so hard to trust him, even though she knew he'd promised her Master not to damage her. A moment later, he stood her up and fastened the belt tight again.

"Listen, I want you to really clean and straighten up the play space today. There's a big party tomorrow. A private party. An orgy," he finally clarified. She swallowed hard. She'd heard about Mephisto's "parties" and the idea had always fascinated her. Thirty or forty people, men and women, unchecked kink and sex. Perhaps...perhaps tomorrow at the party he would let her fly around the room, so to speak. Release her from her enforced denial. She couldn't quite keep the hopeful speculation from her face.

"You're going to be fucked, yes. A lot," he said. "But no, you won't yet be permitted to come. I'll let everybody know. And girl, you won't want to be punished in front of everyone if you screw up. So beware. It might be best if we did a little more edging practice tonight."

Mephisto pinched her nipples, slapping her breasts lightly, while she fervently prayed to never have to endure edging "practice" again. "You know, I might not permit you to come at all until you're returned to your Master. What a gift that would be for him, no? To return you absolutely wild with horniness. Maybe he'd find he liked you that way. I could give him lots of advice about an effective denial program. And that harness is going home with you and him. Hopefully he'll make good use of it."

She blinked, barely restraining herself from shaking her head in horror. *No.* Master would never... Master loved to see her come... He would never... Would he? She hated that Mephisto appeared amused by her panic, and stuffed down those feelings, returning her face to an equivocal mask.

"Nice try, kitten. But everything you think and feel is written on your face, clear as daylight." He slapped her ass. "Now get going. I better not find one speck of dust."

* * * * *

She cleaned until dinnertime, trying not to imagine the various equipment she polished being used at the upcoming party. Being used on *her*. She ached to be released from the harness, to be touched and used by Mephisto, but at the same time she dreaded it.

But Mephisto made no more mention of edging "practice" as he ate and absently fed her while leafing through a local scene magazine. Then he had her sit below his desk, licking and sucking him while he did paperwork and answered emails. She only half-attended to him, part of her mind thinking back to the last time she'd sucked him off under there, when her Master had just left her.

Master.

She touched the cool metal of her collar as she serviced Mephisto, her other Master. The Master she served with her mind, but not her heart. No, her heart was already taken.

Mephisto reached down and slapped her cheek lightly, a silent reminder to focus. She applied herself to her task, drawing a shuddering orgasm from him at long last. She was tired of the taste of latex, and the feel of it inside her when he took her. She yearned for Master's taste and Master's warmth. Master's hardness and his semen on her tongue. Mephisto seemed to have forgotten her, so after she removed his condom with gentle fingers, she laid down at his feet huddled into a curled ball. She dared to run her fingers over the smooth leather of her harness, between her legs and up over her hips. God, she missed coming. She missed talking, too. Mephisto had taken privileges away, privileges she had always taken for granted. It had challenged her submission, and more than once, made her question whether she was even meant to be a slave.

But of course she was meant to be a slave. Just not *his* slave. Some irritating voice in her mind said, *But you still like him. You want him.* She did want him. She wanted his intensity, his sensuality, his intelligence. She wanted to serve him because he demanded it. She rebelled because she so often fell short.

But did she really fall short? She hadn't come in days, not since that one time she'd lost control the first day he edged her. But her mind—her attitude—fell short at times. She pledged to herself to do better. She was a good slave. She wanted Mephisto to think so. She wanted to believe it herself.

"Come, girl," she heard him say. His laptop clicked shut and she scooted out from under the table, crawling behind him back to his bedroom. She watched his ass as he walked, swaggered really. His confidence was so compelling—as was his gorgeous physique. *Don't get turned on.* No matter what he planned, she knew carnal release was not on the menu for her tonight.

He had her stand in the bathroom as he inspected the few unhealed nicks from last night's punishment with the whip. He took off her harness and washed her himself in the shower. He was so much larger than her, and his golden nakedness was intimidating in the enclosed space. His hands moved over her skin, surging into all her naughty crevices, washing away the evidence of a day of unassuaged arousal. She clung to him, her fingers braced against his iron arms. He was so breathtaking, his abs a neat, defined lattice. His chest was smooth power capped with broad shoulders that looked like they could hold up the world. She wanted to wash him too, wanted to run her fingers over every inch of his body. With a half-smile, he handed her the soap.

She took it, blushing under the stream of warm water. He had told her *Everything you think and feel is written on your face, clear as daylight.* She decided she would just stop trying to hide anything from him. The more she tried to hide, the more it seemed he dissected her every thought. Not being able to speak seemed to make her more, not less, transparent. With words, she could dissemble and spout pretty phrases. Without words, she was an open book.

She soaped him up, enjoying the feel of his skin under her fingers. She wondered when he would let her talk again. Was that another thing to be denied until her Master returned for her? She didn't miss the words as much as the sexual release, but she didn't want to forget how to use her voice.

She gazed up at him, framing the question in her mind, to see if he would somehow hear and answer the way he'd uncannily done so many times already. But he only stared back down at her, his lips parted in a faint smile. Her fingers trailed down his stomach, stopping just above his steadily hardening cock. He lowered his head to hers and kissed her. She shivered, even in the warm steam of the shower stall. His lips parted hers, and his tongue played across hers in a teasing motion. She moaned softly, nipping at him and feathering her fingers over the ridges of his abs and the indents of his iliac furrows.

He made a low growling sound that resonated in her chest. She grew bolder, pressing her breasts against his chest, feeling the delicious slide of her nipples against his skin. His hands were roving over her back, then up to squeeze her shoulders. Then down…down to caress her sore ass cheeks. He took her ass in his hands and closed his fingers on it, then slipped one thick digit down from the back to tease the entrance of her pussy. She danced around on her toes at the brief, fleeting contact, pressing closer to him, wanting more. She heard his soft chuckle of approval. *The denial is just a tool for winding you up so I can watch you writhe and wriggle for me.*

She moaned again in her throat, missing words, missing the ability to beg him. *Please fuck me,* she thought. *Please, I'll do anything. Just fuck me and let me come.*

He turned off the water abruptly, and Molly stood dripping. Dripping water from her hair and the contours of her body, but dripping between the legs too. He gave her an assessing look. "You horny little piece of ass. You wanton sex doll. Keep a hold of yourself." He pulled her from the shower and toweled her off roughly, then pushed her ahead of him back into the bedroom. "On the bed, face down. No, wait a minute."

He opened a drawer and pulled out a folded piece of plain ivory cloth. She watched with a sense of anxiety as he spread it over the bed sheets, right in the center. "Okay, now," he said, drawing back. "Face down."

Molly swallowed hard and did as she was told.

"Arms out, legs spread."

She reached her arms out toward each post of the bed and spread her thighs. He bound her with leather cuffs already affixed to his bed frame, leaving just enough room for her to twist a little—by design, she was sure. He left her then, looking through drawers that contained god knew what. As she watched with wide eyes, he threw a white taper candle on the bed, "hot" lubricant, and a slender black crop. And something else she knew all too well. A slim silver vibrator.

She made a tiny whimper of a sound, which only resulted in a desultory snort of amusement from him.

"Don't worry, kitten. You'll enjoy this very much. Well, parts of it." He knelt beside her on the bed, working a thin sheen of the cinnamon lube onto the base of the candle. "Arch your hips up."

The candle slid into her asshole, deeply enough to make her uncomfortable, but not nearly as uncomfortable as when she heard the match. "Be still," he warned when she tried to turn. He placed a hand on the small of her back and she buried her face in the sheets as he—she assumed—lit the candle. Her ass was feeling warm and twitchy from the lube. The candle was slightly greater in diameter than a typical dinner candle, and that too made her want to squirm and shift. Her clit was already pulsing. He pressed harder on the small of her back. "I want absolutely no movement. At least for a moment."

She obeyed, clenching her fists and willing herself to stillness. Then, without warning, he pinched the sensitive skin on the inside of her thigh, and she yelped and shifted jerkily. Immediately she felt a spray of hot stinging pricks across her ass cheeks and upper thighs. She cried out, not realizing at first what he'd done to her. She thought of barbed wire, vampire gloves, needles. He put his hand on her back again. "Be still."

She sobbed softly, and her mind returned to coherence. The wax. He was holding her still while the candle burned down and the top filled with a pool of hot liquid. The predicament was obvious. If she stayed still, it slid harmlessly down the side of the candle. If she moved, it splashed out onto her skin. Already the first volley of drips had dried and cooled, but the memory of the pain lingered. She just had to be still. She *had* to be still. She felt onerously burdened and unbearably controlled. *Don't talk. Don't beg. Don't move. Don't shift. Don't come.* And above it all, his immovable hand pressed to her back, fixing her to the bed by pure power.

Then he released her, and the responsibility was hers. *Don't move. Don't move.* She saw the crop disappear from the bed beside her, heard the whistling sound of it in the air, just giving her milliseconds to brace—

But stillness was impossible as the fiery pain sliced across the middle of her thighs. She jerked and felt the spill of hot wax land just at the apex of her leg, below her ass cheek. Two horrible pains to process at once, and nothing to do but lie still to prevent more pain. *Mephisto*, she wanted to cry. *Demon!* He was so evil. But in the midst of her pain her clit was alive with longing. She turned her head, knowing more pain was coming. He was making her wait for it. Another crack of the crop against her left cheek, and she pulled away, spraying wax across her right buttock. Two types of burn, but the wax burn was worse because it spilled and spread in an unpredictable pattern that was never the same.

His hand was on her back again, soothing her. Making her wait while the hot liquid built up again. Her pussy ached, empty and unused, while her ass clenched on the waxy instrument of her own torture. "This is fun, isn't it?" he asked lightly.

Her answering moan of protest was met by the soft buzz of the vibrator being switched on. "Now, this will be *more* fun." She felt his fingers parting her pussy lips, and she trembled with the effort it took to stay still. He nudged the tip of the vibrator against her clitoris, barely touching her. She could be still for this. She could endure it, with self control. The low hum was a pleasant tingle, arousing but not unbearable.

But as ever, he was patient. He swirled it around, a trail of teasing sensation, and then centered it again on her clit. She took quick, panting breaths. She could be still...but if she didn't move away from the delicious contact, her body would come with or without her intention. She whined, pleading in the only way she could for his mercy, but he only started the swirling, taunting movements again. She waited, steeling herself, trying to will the arousal away, trying to deny the peak that was coming, but then...

She groaned and jerked her hips away, feeling wax spray across the backs of both her thighs. She suffered not just the pain of the wax droplets, but the horrible physical frustration of the denied orgasm.

"Good girl," he said, brushing a hand down her back before pinning her still again. "Such an obedient slave. Your Master is pleased."

So let me up, she thought. *Please take the candle out and let me up. Then please stick your cock in my pussy. Or my ass. Wherever. Make this ache go away.*

Buzzz... A moment later the vibrator was back again. Three more times he brought her to the edge, forcing her to punish herself doubly by pulling away from the very orgasm she desperately craved. Her buttocks and thighs were spattered with wax, some even dripping down into the sensitive cleft between her ass cheeks. The last time, she burst into tears of frustration. Not because she'd missed another orgasm—she was resigned to that torture, as much as it plagued her. No, it was because she'd *almost* given up that time. She had been mere seconds from just allowing herself to come after all these many days of denying herself for him.

To come at this point, before he allowed it, would crush her completely, not to mention disappoint him beyond bearing. Perhaps there was something in her miserable crying that moved him, or alerted him to the fact that she could not be wound up further, because he switched off the evil silver vibrator. She felt the whisper of his breath across her ass as he blew out the candle. The tension of stress left her body in inching degrees, so she felt for the first time the scratchiness of the linen square underneath her, and the softer feel of his sheets beneath her cheek. They smelled of him. With the panic and tension gone, her senses came alive. And still the arousal remained, a nagging weight in her pelvis. An empty, excruciating longing not to be fulfilled.

He backed away, undoing the cuffs at her ankles. Then he was back, the bed dipping behind her. He lifted her legs, sliding his knees beneath them. He grasped her hips and she felt the press of his cock against her aching pussy. He stretched her open, touching her deep inside, filling her to the hilt. The candle still invaded her ass with its persistent sting, a sensation made more noticeable as his cock rubbed against it through the walls of her channels. It was an odd, overwhelming sensation, more provocative then pleasurable.

As he fucked her, he manipulated the candle, working it in and out, up and back, all to the soundtrack of her whimpers, moans, and guttural lust sounds. When at last he came, she was aroused but not frantic, and so she was able to enjoy the feeling of his cock pulsing inside her. She was able to hear his jerky breaths and the low moan in his throat, rather than her own internal monologue of need. She absorbed his heightened final thrusts with a different kind of satisfaction—that of a slave who has denied her own desires and wishes in service to her Master.

Afterward, he stayed in her a long while, still toying with the candle and lazily stroking her back. Now and again he peeled and flicked pieces of wax off her. She took each touch, each pang of fleeting arousal, as another gift of her slavehood. She could tell by the tenderness of his fingers that he was pleased. Finally he stood to discard his condom and free her of the candle's intrusion. He removed the cloth and took her to the bathroom to clean up. He peeled the remaining wax off himself with deft fingers. She fought against feelings of love and affection for him, but when he was so tender and gentle...

When he was satisfied that she was cleaned up to his specifications, he took her hands in his and kissed each one. His eyes gazed into hers with a strange intensity of feeling. "I'm very proud of you, kitten."

She swallowed, flushing, feeling suddenly close to tears. She wanted to say that it was all his doing...that he had taught her, explained it all to her, and that it finally made sense even if it *was* terribly difficult.

He led her back to the bedroom and detached the cuffs from the bed, putting them back on her wrists. Then he clipped them with another length of chain through the ring in her collar so she couldn't lower them even to her waist. "I trust you more now," he said. "But sometimes in sleep even the best slaves forget."

She expected to be led to the cage but he pointed to his bed. She complied, trying not to reveal her surprise or the flutter in her chest. When he climbed in beside her and pulled her back against him, she settled into his embrace of evident approval, supremely content. His warmth and power was like a bastion around her, and she knew she would do anything, give up anything to please him. Just as she would for her other Master.

Mephisto had finally mastered her. God help her. She drifted off in his arms, not even thinking once about how many days she had left.

THE FIFTH DAY

They slept late the next day, Mephisto awakening with mutters of all the things he needed to get accomplished for the party. After a hurried breakfast, he led her back in the bedroom and ordered her to bend over the bed. She expected the dreaded harness, but he brought a substantial butt plug instead. She groaned inwardly as he lubed it—without tingling lube, thankfully. But still...

"I know many of my guests will want to use your ass tonight, kitten," he said at her sigh of resignation. He spread her legs apart with his feet on the floor and landed a couple sharp slaps on her ass cheeks. "Open for Master."

She braced herself and pressed back against the toy as he drove it forward. He worked it in and out, slapping her ass again when it didn't slide in. Finally, with a numbing, aching burn, the plug popped in and her sphincter closed around the wide base. The flange rested between her ass cheeks, a reminder of her status and a visible humiliation.

"Here," he said, pointing to the place at the foot of the bed where he often left her tethered—the place easily visible from his camera. She knelt, feeling the fullness of the plug as she sat back on her ankles, a fullness that triggered a predictable low throb between her legs. He gathered his keys and cell phone and then stopped by his bookshelf of erotica in the corner. Molly had scanned the shelves the few times she'd had a free moment in his bedroom, finding many classics and many lesser known titles as well. He picked out a small book and placed it on the bed beside her.

"Some reading for you," he said with a smile. "Don't want you to be bored."

He sauntered off, not even looking back at her. Such freedom he enjoyed, and here she sat, leashed to a bed, bisected by a massive butt plug. She smiled to herself. She wouldn't have changed places with him for the world.

A moment later, she reached to look at the book he'd left her. Some torrid fantasy-sex-slave novel. It was exactly the type of book she used to read before she started actually living the lifestyle, and she knew just from scanning the back cover that it would turn her on to a dangerous degree. She placed it back on the bed, determined to resist temptation. She had no confining harness on to keep her honest, and the toy in her ass was already prodding her arousal level into the caution zone. No doubt he'd left the book to create another predicament for her. Avoid boredom, but deal with mounting horniness, or be bored but not so horny. What a talented sadist he was.

She sat and thought about other things. Her mind was quieter, much more serene since he'd explained the purpose behind his treatment of her. She knew she shouldn't have to depend on explanations and reassurances to prop up her submission, a lesson she was still learning. But for the moment, at least, she felt herself in a comfortable place. She thought about Master and how near she was to seeing him again. Today was

Wednesday. He would return for her sometime on Friday. She closed her eyes and daydreamed about his blue eyes, his voice and the sensation of his touch. She knew she'd grown in her experiences and in her submission this week, which is what he'd wanted of her. She would use what she'd learned—about denial, about unselfishness—and apply it to her service of him.

Time passed quickly as she thought about the various ways to do that, although her stomach was rumbling by the time she finally heard him out in the other room. She smiled, unable to disguise her pleasure to see him when he came into the bedroom. He returned her smile, but then frowned at the book lying on the bed.

"I expected to find you reading. What did you think of the book?"

All the self-satisfied pride she'd felt about her progress in Mephisto's keeping dissipated in a sick, sinking feeling of disaster. She only shook her head, unable to answer his question.

"You didn't read it? At all?" She bit her lip and bowed her head, hating this horrible moment and the irritated disbelief in his voice. "Why do you think I left it there beside you? As I said, it was reading for you. Reading I expected you to do."

She was mute, forbidden to speak anyway. But if she could have spoken, what would she have said? *I'm sorry. I didn't know. I was stupid. Forgive me.* Apologies. Excuses. None of it took away her mistake. She was so preoccupied with trying *not* to get horny, that she hadn't even considered the fact that he'd given her the book expecting her to read it. She did the only thing she could think to do, which was to slowly lean forward and press her forehead to the floor in a pathetic plea for his forgiveness. For the punishment she knew she deserved.

She heard the springs on the bed, felt herself lifted across his hard lap. She clung to his leg as he started raining stinging blows on her bottom, accompanied by a lecture meant to sting just as much.

"How forward of you, slave, to just assume a choice. I don't give you choices. I give you instructions." *Smack. Smack. Smack.* He pressed the plug deeper in her ass, twisting it viciously so she whimpered and strained against him. "I give the instructions in this relationship. You follow them. If I take the time to pick out a fucking book and give it to you, you fucking—" *Smack.* "Read." *Smack.* "It. Don't you?" *Smack. Smack. Smack.*

The pain was so awful. His hand was like a paddle, only stingy-er. She wanted to kick her legs, to pull away and plead for respite, but she forced herself to lie still and accept the angry blows raining on her ass. She still cried, dripping hot, copious tears against the dark denim of his jeans. How could she have screwed up so badly, just when she was starting to make progress under his dominion?

The tempo of the blows increased and she cried harder, tensing her ass cheeks as if that might somehow save her, but it only reminded her of the acute invasion of the plug in her bottom. He stood with a tsk and pushed her face down on the bed. She heard the whisking sound of a belt sliding free of its loops at the same time she felt his knee press down against the middle of her back. She cried out as the doubled-over belt seared across her ass. The book was beside her face, taunting her. Another shockingly painful blow, and another. "From now on, you don't do what *you* decide you prefer. You do what *I* tell you to do." *Whack!* "Open the book, now, and start reading."

With a stifled sob, Molly grabbed the book and opened to the first page, stammering out the title and the author's name, crying hysterically as the belt fell again. She hadn't said anything in days, and the syllables sounded garbled.

"Louder, so I can hear you!"

She read it again, crying, trying to enunciate through tears. She turned to the next page and started to read the story aloud, swiping the blurry wetness from her eyes so she could see the print. As she read, the whipping continued and she had no avenue to escape it. His knee still held her firmly pressed to the bed. She wailed, feeling turned inside out, trying to focus on reading the words she could so easily have read in his absence. At last, by the end of the fourth excruciating page, he flung the belt down beside her.

"Keep reading," he barked when she paused. "Read the whole damn thing. Out loud. Don't move until you're done. You deserve worse, but I want my guests to have a chance to mark you at the party," he said with a final frustrated slap to her rear.

She read, barely able to remember the basics of the story in her misery, but fortunately she remembered enough to answer the handful of questions he asked her a couple hours later.

"Put the book on the shelf, and then return to kneel here before me," he said after he quizzed her.

Her legs were sore and shaky after her long time bent over the bed, but she wobbled over and reshelved the book. She turned with her eyes downcast and fell to her knees before him. He was already sheathed, and she opened without resisting as he pressed his cock to her mouth. He fucked her face, holding her by the back of the neck lest she be so foolish as to pull away. But she didn't. She let him use her, a limp vessel of shame and self-loathing.

Afterward he tipped her face up, scrutinizing her. If he was looking for evidence of remorse, he surely saw it, for she felt remorse down to every nerve and pore of her body. She opened her mouth to speak, but he silenced her. "No. No talking. I don't want it. Just listen to me. You screwed up, and you were punished for it. You're forgiven, but don't ever assume a choice again when it's not expressly given. Nod if you understand me."

She nodded avidly, trying to infuse all her sorrow and penitence into her gaze. He drew a thumb across her cheek, then leaned down to kiss her lips, cradling her face in his hands. He pulled away, staring down at her. "We won't let this derail the progress you've made. The party's starting soon, and I want you at your best. You'll serve in whatever way is requested. Everyone there will be a trusted friend or client who can be depended on to follow the rules. You play your role...slave and plaything. And obviously," he added with a warning, "you are not to come. You will exist tonight for others' pleasure, not your own. Nod if you understand me."

She nodded again, and he led her out to the kitchen to eat, and then to wash up and have the plug removed. He buckled his own house collar around her neck above her Master's—a signal she was club property to be shared—and led her out to the main area just as the other help was starting to arrive.

* * * * *

Molly was kept in a "harem" with other girls and boys available to be used. She recognized one girl, Lila, from the first night, and the girl who had locked her in the cage the second day, but Jamie was not among the small group of male subs. There were ten of them all together, three males and seven females kept in a kind of corral set up in the corner. The tops were all males, and she counted twenty-six at the height of the party. They were all fit and attractive, although some were significantly older or younger than Mephisto's age, which Molly guessed was around thirty-five. One commonality the tops all shared was that they were all strikingly virile. As she looked around in the dim black light, with the house music throbbing, she thought she'd never seen such an impressive collection of hard, upstanding cocks all in one place.

The subs were naked from the start, excepting collars that identified their status. The men who'd been invited to play with them stripped within the first half hour or so, after a drink or two. Molly thought she could have used a drink for courage, but the only drinks provided for the bottoms were communal dog bowls of tap water, which at least was kept cool and frequently refreshed.

Mephisto stood, nude too in all his glory, overseeing the collection of submissive bodies, using the tap of a whip to force backs straighter and breasts more suggestively outthrust. Molly's pussy was seeping from the open, speculative regard of the males in attendance. She cast furtive glances at the various faces. None of them were masked—Mephisto didn't permit it, per club rules. He said he didn't allow anything to go on in his club that a person couldn't do to another person face-to-face. Mephisto also didn't allow photographs, and kept a tight group of well-known clientele so there were no worries about infiltration or invasion of privacy. Molly knew all this from things Master had told her. She also realized most of the men in the room were probably very successful at whatever they did, if not filthy rich.

That, too, aroused her. Success. Aptitude. And of course, the requisite virility all these man shared. When they started circling the corral of available bodies, stroking and pinching, groping and considering, Molly wanted to be selected. She couldn't deny that selfish desire.

But they were all selected eventually. Repeatedly. The top-to-bottom ratio was purposely calculated to force each sub to nearly constant use. The play space soon filled with the sounds of pleasure and pain, torment and impact. There were voices, orders and instructions, some ribald jokes and dirty talk, but only from the dominant side. Molly soon realized that her speech restriction training had been in preparation for this, for becoming a silent, available vessel for the pleasure of Mephisto's guests.

The first hand that reached for her belonged to a sleepy-eyed man with auburn hair flopping over his forehead. He murmured something against her ear that she couldn't hear, but she understood the nudge of his hand well enough. She fell to her knees, taking the condom he placed in her hand and rolling it onto his thick cock. He was pale like Master, not dark like Mephisto. She fellated him there, in front of everyone, as similar scenes took place around them. She heard the moans of one of the male subs, and wicked-sounding smacks. A girl to her left was being fucked in the ass on all fours. A moment later she felt hands on her ass and felt herself rearranged. She didn't dare stop sucking the man before her to look back, but she moaned around his dick as she felt her ass cheeks parted and a cold dab of lube smeared across her tiny hole.

She sucked in breath, opening her throat as someone impaled her ass. The man before her pulled her hair to refocus her and she deep-throated him as she struggled to adjust to the pain of the invasion behind her. Her moans seemed to drive both men on, and soon the man before her pulled away and took off his condom, yanking her upright and jetting copious streams of cum over her breasts.

The man behind her grappled with her, instructing her to rub the cum into her breasts and moan while he fucked her. She obeyed, closing her eyes and clenching around his cock. She tried to open herself to his driving assault, to the uncomfortable, humbling sensation of having her ass used so capriciously. The acute feeling of being dominated, and his animalistic grunts soon had her bucking back against him in willing surrender. He came with a rough gasp and a deep thrust, pinching her nipples painfully.

He pulled away with a stinging slap to her ass. She barely had time to turn and see the man who'd fucked her when another man lifted her from her knees. She was led to one of the dungeon's many crosses and shackled, spread-eagled. She was flogged on the back and thighs by two men in a row, a stinging torment that left her warmed and trembling. They chose to fuck her afterward, one man finishing in her pussy and the other choosing to use her ass. She hung from her bonds as they took turns, powerless and conquered. Used. Horny. She ached to rub her clit against the slick, hard wood before her but she didn't dare. *Control yourself. Don't disappoint your Master.*

She was returned to the corral for just a moment, catching only a glance of the various decadent sexual acts around her before another gentleman grabbed her wrist. Mephisto watched while accepting oral service from a girl at his feet. Molly thought he might have winked at her, but maybe she'd imagined it.

She tripped along behind the slim, dark-haired man dragging her to a spanking bench. He shackled her on her hands and knees. She felt a moment of panic when he restrained both her ankles *and* her thighs, cuffing them and linking them to unseen attachment points. She was completely immobilized, a terrifying feeling, especially as he went to the wall and returned with a rattan cane. She was grateful now for the restraints, but panicked too. The first slice of the cane was horrible, spreading fire, and she cried out. He waited as she squirmed in her bonds, no doubt enjoying the spectacle of her struggle. She wished she could reach back and rub her sizzling cheeks, but then another stroke fell, and another. She wailed and jerked at each fresh assault of the painful implement. He finally put it down, but only to fetch a pair of adjustable nipple clamps from the club's vast selection.

He returned, tipping her face up and wiping some of the tears from her cheeks. She gazed up into light green eyes and a sternly handsome face. "I want less noise, girl. Each time you scream and cry like that, I'm going to tighten these clamps more. Understand me?"

She nodded miserably, trying to restrain the hiss that rose to her lips as he closed first one, and then the other of the heavy clamps on her nipples. Her pussy constricted and her clit pulsed from the erotic pangs of pain, but the soreness of her punished ass cheeks kept her from tipping over the edge.

He once again took up his position behind her with the cane. Molly gritted her teeth but each subsequent strike ended up resulting in another turn of the tightening screws, since she couldn't suppress her voice's reaction to the pain of the caning. She sobbed and wiggled in her bonds, desperate for some escape from the torture to her ass and the squeezing clamps on her nipples. At last, the helpless squirming of her bottom seemed to distract him from punishing her. He climbed up on the table behind her and thrust his sheathed cock balls-deep into her dripping pussy. He banged his hips against her aching ass, squeezing her scarlet cheeks. The pain and pleasure merged and again she felt herself climbing, climbing... She pressed her forehead against the vinyl bench. *Don't. Don't. Don't come.*

When he finally released her and returned her to the corner, she sat up on her knees, not even able to rest her ass back on her ankles because it was so tender. She watched the men warily, terrified to be taken by one who wished to spank or cane her again on the too-fresh welts. But the party seemed to be mellowing. The scenes were ratcheting down, becoming more lazy and sensual from their earlier heightened pitch. She had what seemed like twenty or thirty minutes to rest. Perhaps Mephisto, in his effortless grasp of control, engineered it with nothing more than quelling looks to men who considered her.

When one finally claimed her again, it was for more sensual play. The short, compactly built man put a thick, vibrating dildo in her hand and propped her on her knees, ordering her to insert it and masturbate herself. *Tell me to come,* she thought. *Please order me to come.* Surely she couldn't disobey a direct order of one of Mephisto's guests.

But no such order was forthcoming. When she'd worked the dildo deep inside, writhing from the buzzing, shuddering pleasure, he took a fistful of her hair and leaned over her back, driving his cock into her asshole and taking her in jerky short strokes that had her moaning in longing. Oh, God, what it would feel like to come from such fullness and stimulation! She wanted to cry. She wanted to scream. She wanted to disobey. Mephisto strolled past, catching her eye. An unmistakable warning. He watched until the man was finished with her.

Another man took her after that, and then another. She sucked, she fucked, she was filled and brought *almost* to orgasm again and again. Her nipples were pinched and clamped until they throbbed and felt heavier than usual, another reminder of her captive sexuality, her denial of release. She felt like one big aching lump of flesh, crying out for surrender. Then, abruptly, the party ended. The men dressed and headed out, perhaps to a leisurely late dinner or after-orgy drinks.

Mephisto cuffed Molly to one of the crosses, clamped yet again, as he showed the guests out and bundled off the other submissives, thanking them all for their service. Molly stood in her restraints, her chest heaving with each breath, her legs shifting, her pussy aching to be filled, her pelvis aching to come. To reach satisfaction. The dispersing of the guests did nothing to disperse her horniness. He finally returned, taking in her heightened gaze with amused understanding. He tapped her clit, just once, and she almost screamed.

"You're wound so tight, my lovely little slave girl," he murmured. "Would you like me to touch you again?"

She gasped and shook her head, then nodded. But he only chuckled. "I don't think so. I'm going to release you now." He uncuffed her hands so they flopped down at her sides. Again, he tapped and stroked her clit just a moment. When he stopped, she sobbed softly. She thought she would explode if she couldn't just...if she couldn't just...

Her hand slid toward her mons. She only meant to rest it nearby—

He slapped it away. "No."

She tried again, just to touch her clit...not even stroke it. Just touch it once. For one second. She couldn't bear it—

He took her arms in a hard grip and slapped her face. "I said no." He raised his hand again, but she shook her head, coming to her senses. He was still frowning. "You were such a good girl at the party. But you're not being a very good girl now. Put your hands on your head."

She sobbed but obeyed him. He released her ankles and unclamped her nipples. Even the agonizing rush of blood to the tips of her breasts didn't dampen the need she felt. He marched her to use the bathroom and shower, giving her a perfunctory cleaning with her hands cuffed behind her back. He used nothing but a spray of ice cold water on her pussy and engorged clit so even that contact was denied. But at least the icy water cut through her mindless desperation and brought her boiling lust down to a bearable simmer. Then she began to feel the shame. She cried when he presented the harness, both dildos coated liberally with the sadistic oil. "You were doing so well," he said, shaking his head with a grimace before he bent her over to drive the dildos home.

When do I become broken? was all she could think in answer. She felt broken as he shoved her into the underbed cage with her hands still cuffed behind her back and the harness cinched tightly closed. For an hour or more she ached and burned, all the while knowing he was lounging on the bed above her. At some point, when she sobbed aloud, he banged the side of the cage and told her to sleep.

THE SIXTH DAY

She must have slept, although she thought it impossible, because she awakened to the rattle of the bed-cage's bars and Mephisto staring into her eyes.

"Are you better now?" he asked, in a voice neither kind nor accusing.

She nodded, wanting to hide her face in shame, but her hands were still cuffed behind her. He pulled her out. He was already showered, while she felt grungy and exhausted. He removed her harness and took her to the kitchen, forcing her to eat when she resisted. She did begin to feel slightly better by the end of the meal. He cleared his plates himself, then left the kitchen, leaving her kneeling and unsupervised. The implied restoration of trust bolstered her a little. He returned with a pair of jeans, a tee shirt and pale green sweater.

"I believe these are your size."

She took the clothes he handed her in surprise.

"Yes, we're going out. It's a really beautiful day and you haven't gotten much exercise this week. Put these on. No panties, and no bra. I don't want anything between me and you but these articles of clothing."

She stood and drew on the comfortable garments. They did fit well. The shirt was a little flimsy and snug across her chest, but the sweater was thick and cozy for the chilly early spring weather. Mephisto fingered her collar, removing the O-ring that betrayed the decorative band's true purpose.

"Vanilla enough, I guess," he said with a smile.

His relaxed mood soothed her in turn. In his sleek black sports car, on the way to wherever he was taking her, he reiterated the importance of his orgasm denial regimen. He also praised her overall performance at the party, if not her breakdown at the end. So she was left feeling, at the very least, forgiven.

One more day.

Master would come for her tomorrow. After that, Mephisto wouldn't control her any more—not her orgasms, her speech, anything. She tried to convince herself she would be relieved to wash her hands of his control, but the truth was, she'd forged a connection to Mephisto. She'd truly come to think of him as her Master, and to admire his charisma and control, if not the trials he put her through.

He drove her to a Seattle city park, and they took a brisk walk around the jogging path with all the other people enjoying the unseasonably beautiful weather. She wondered what they looked like to the vanilla eye. A handsome man in black, obviously a progressive type with his dreadlocks and piercings. She, the more conservative-looking girl in the jeans and green sweater, long curly hair occasionally blowing across her face in the breeze.

"You look pretty without makeup," he said. He held her hand briefly, then released it. They stopped at a snack bar, and he bought ice cream and popcorn. He shared the swirled cone with her first, and she savored the treat. Ice cream was something her Master allowed her only occasionally, and never this soft, creamy variety she used to enjoy so much as a child. He watched her take each delicate lick, a gleam in his eye. She laughed softly, swiping a drip from her chin.

"Take more, if you like it."

He ended up giving her most of the cone in the end, while he crunched on the popcorn and threw some to the birds swooping up and down. Master hadn't taken her out to a park like this in years. He took her to plays, concerts, and hundred-dollar dinners regularly, but not this. Of course, Master was a busy man, and not very outdoorsy. They lived in a high rise downtown, where sprawling parks like this were hard to come by. It wasn't a big thing to give up. Still, she wished she could save the feeling of the breeze in her hair and the sweet taste of the ice cream melting against her tongue. And the look Mephisto was giving her.

Silence came easily now. There were a lot of things she would have liked to ask him, a lot of things she would have chatted about, but silence seemed more suitable between them somehow. Silence easily turned physical, while words were mental. He pulled her into his lap and thrust salty fingers into her mouth, letting her lick off the grease of the popcorn. She giggled a little, and he stuck his other hand up under her tee shirt, beneath her sweater, pinching and stroking her nipples. They instantly went taut.

He did it for a long while, turning her against him to hide his activity from passersby. Her pussy grew warm and wet pressed against his thigh. She slid a hand around his neck—a forward, unrequested embrace—but he didn't correct her. She rested her face against his cheek, making tiny, faint noises of pleasure. He pinched harder and she made a whisper of a moan.

He squeezed her breast then and kissed her, hard, grasping a handful of her hair in his other hand. She felt his own secret groan against her lips. He pulled away and looked around the crowded park in frustration. "My own orgasm denial," he said ruefully. "For once, I feel your pain."

He took her hand and they walked again, past the busiest part of the park to a wooded area. There, behind a curtain of thick brush and bushes, she knelt and served him, taking his cock in her mouth as the birds sang and squirrels chattered in the background. She heard some voices now and again, but they weren't close. Even if they had been close, even if they'd stood and watched her, she wouldn't have stopped. Her mind was fixed on her Master, on her Master's cock and balls, and the soft encouraging noises he made that drove her until he found his satisfaction. He stumbled away from her, zipping up again. He handed her the condom and she buried it a few inches deep under some loose dirt and dry, decayed leaves. She imagined for a moment she was planting Mephisto trees, to grow up strong and tall and dominant like him.

"Silly girl," he said, watching with a bemused look as she carefully covered over the rubber. But as Mephisto pointed out, she'd earned a degree in environmental studies. She knew that condoms could be harmful to wildlife. She probably should have carried it back to a trash can, but she didn't have anything to wrap it in. With all the people in the park, carrying it swinging from her fingertips would have been taking humiliation a bit too far.

Oh, the moral conundrums of a slave.

He took her hand again, leading her out from the trees along a path he seemed to know well. Soon she heard the low rushing of water, and they came out at the bank of a small creek. It was sandy on the bottom, with large rocks jutting up and creating criss-crossing eddies and currents in the water. The shore was lined by more low bushes and trees. Molly remembered the names of most of the trees. Her area of specialization had been water and wetlands.

She wondered how he knew that.

She had no doubt he'd brought her here purposely. The speculative way he stood back and observed her told her that. Well, what did he expect her to do? Start taking water samples? Search for evidence of animal activity? Map the varieties of marine life? The creek had a good amount of minnows in it, which told her a lot about the health of the local environment. She hated that she analyzed it as she stood there. She used to wade these types of creeks in vinyl thigh boots on misty mornings, in sweaters and jeans just like the ones she had on. She used to measure amoebic activity and chemical levels. Used to. *Used to.*

The breeze rustled the trees, a sound that had always seemed to her to convey the power of the earth. The trees were budding, tender new shoots with the advent of spring. She used to know all this, love all this. All this used to rule her world. Until Master.

When the tears blurring her eyes finally started to roll down her cheeks, Mephisto took her home.

* * * * *

It was only a weak moment, she told herself. The beautiful day. The ice cream. The people in the park, carefree and laughing. She loved her life with Master, much more than she loved her old work or her old life. *Much* more. Still, she felt unsettled. Had Mephisto taken her there to hurt her? The silence that seemed to suit them before, now seemed sinister. She wanted to ask him to explain his purpose, his motives, but enforced silence was a wall between them.

For his part, he was thoughtful and close-lipped on the ride home and through the afternoon. He kept her busy cleaning the play space and doing other mindless household tasks. When she finished them, he set her up in the kitchen with an ironing board and a pile of clothes. Molly wasn't great at ironing. In fact, she was terrible. She always seemed to create more wrinkles than she smoothed out. Back when she bought her own clothes—back when she wore clothes—she always bought the wrinkle-free kind. At Master's home, Mrs. Jernigan took care of the ironing. More things she'd taken for granted. As much as it had challenged her, she knew this time with Mephisto had been invaluable in opening her eyes.

She did her best with the shirts and pants, wrangling with the collars and plackets. She eyed the starch and decided to take her chances without it. Mephisto was sitting out at his desk-table right next door. Perhaps she ought to just break her speech restriction and tell him she didn't know how to iron. But then she'd see that awful derision. *Pleasure slave. Not very useful, are you?* But if she ruined his clothes... Another slave conundrum.

She was still arguing with herself, pulling at the iron cord and trying to flatten down a collar, when she yelped at a searing, burning pain. She'd brushed the inside of her forearm against the iron. It was already going numb and tingling. Some instinctive part of her brain thought of cold water. She flew to the sink, fumbling with the faucet handle and thrusting her arm under the soothing stream.

"What happened?"

Mephisto was beside her, no doubt alerted by her screech of pain. He grabbed her arm, staring down at the skin that was already puckering into blisters. "Fuck!" He put it back under the water. "Fuck!" he shouted again so she flinched. His dark eyes bored into her, frightening her. "Did you do this on purpose?" He shook her arm as he yelled at her. "Did you?"

She made a negative jerk of her head, his question confusing her. Burn herself on purpose?

"Talk to me, damn it!"

"You put me on speech restriction," she pointed out, pulling her arm away from his rough grasp.

He gave her a quick, sharp slap across the cheek. She didn't know if he was slapping her for burning herself or slapping her for pulling away from him, but he seemed to get a handle on himself after that. His lips twisted into a frown and he glared at her.

"Forget the speech restriction. How the fuck did this happen?"

"It was an accident. I'm sorry!"

"I promised your Master no permanent damage," he said. "No scars!"

Again she stared in miserable, tongue-tied helplessness. He unplugged the iron with a jerky movement and steered her into the bedroom. He ran her arm under the water some more and then got a towel and dried her burn with a gentleness belied by his anger. It stood out now in red, stark relief against the pale skin of her forearm, but it was only a couple inches long. "Jesus Christ," he yelled again as he wrapped the burn in a loose gauze bandage. "He's going to kill me."

"But it was my fault, Master," she said, more out of desperation to soothe him than contradict him. Still, she braced for another slap. It didn't come. He ran his hands through his dreadlocks and then pulled her back out to his work table.

"Sit here. Just sit here and don't move."

She heard him on the phone in the bedroom. Talking to her Master? She couldn't make out any of what he said. She ran her fingers over the gauze on her arm. The pain wasn't even that bad anymore. She laid her head on the smooth wood surface of the table and listened to the faint humming sound of his laptop at the other end. Even after he stopped talking on the phone, he didn't come out of his room for a while. She sat still and silent, feeling like a boat set adrift. Long minutes ticked by.

When he finally returned, he had that familiar but unfathomable expression on his face. She looked up at him and thought, *he really is so handsome. It's really a sin, how handsome he is.* But he still looked deeply unhappy.

"Master," she said. "It—it already feels better."

The stare went on. The weighing, the consideration. Finally he spoke in a soft but authoritative voice. "I need to see you in the bedroom."

She followed, not sure what awaited her. It could be punishment, but she hoped not. As soon as he turned to her inside the door, she knew it wasn't. He stood close to her and ran his fingers through her hair. He lifted her injured arm and kissed her wrist, just above the loosely wrapped bandage.

"Your Master misses you," he said quietly.

"Oh. You talked to him?"

"Yes."

Yes, of course he had. Why was she asking stupid questions? Perhaps because she'd finally been released from speech restriction. Perhaps because of the way he was running his fingers down over her breasts, across her belly. Perhaps it was that look in his eyes just before he lowered his lips to hers and kissed her. Perhaps it was the sight of him stripping off his shirt and dropping his jeans to the floor. Perhaps it was his golden-bronze body, or the magnificence of his cock steadily rising before her. She swallowed, her mouth beginning to water. She started to drop to her knees but he stopped her.

"No."

He nudged her toward the bed, bending her over, tracing the welts that still decorated her ass. He kissed her from the base of her spine up to her nape. She felt his cock bump against the backs of her thighs. He pulled away with a curse, going for a condom. She stood still, her pussy throbbing, aching for his penetration. But when he returned, when he started to enter her, he did so only shallowly.

"Molly..." Her name was a low, resonating note in the silence. She froze, startled to even hear it on his lips. He moved deeper, and she moaned, her skin singing for his touch. He reached beneath her and slid sure fingers between her pussy lips, finding her swollen clit. He pressed it, tapping it in a teasing motion. She arched back against him, hating this pleasure and yet unable to steel herself against it. He played her like an instrument, drawing the notes from her whether she wished it or not. She had her voice now...she might plead and beg for climax if she wanted to. But she didn't want to.

She squeezed around his cock, wanting to be used, wanting to be taken. Wanting to serve.

"Master," she whispered. "I'm yours."

His teeth closed on her neck, biting and then gentling into a nibble. He slid deep in her, pressing her forward onto the bed. Her legs failed and she fell onto her arms. She hissed softly as her burn slid across the sheets. He lifted her, turning her over, and then he came over her like an angel. Like a demon. "Hold onto me," he rasped. "Let me hold you."

He slid over her and she arched beneath him, wrapping her legs around his hips. She grasped his neck with her arms. She twisted fingers in his coarse dreadlocks and pulled, not caring if she hurt him, not caring if he hurt her. He was rough but he was gentle, a revelation of sensual opposites. For a moment she imagined he was not her Master at all, but something even more elemental. Her soul, her spirit. The other half of what she was. A perfect fit, like some universal puzzle piece. His cock was the key that opened her. She fell completely open to him, whispering words she couldn't remember that she wasn't even sure made sense.

He pulled her closer, one hand splayed across her back, pressing her against the twist and clench of his abs. All the built-up, denied desire swirled and built inside her. She was that little airplane, twisting, turning. He was the rubber band, wrapped tighter and tighter around her. Slowly, she came to realize that the dynamic between them was different, transformed. Her gaze flew to his and she saw expectant encouragement there. Her heart gave a throb, and her pelvis lurched forward against him. Nerves and synapses snapped to life, and she understood that she didn't need to push down the arousal this time. Didn't have to ignore it, hate it. He was giving her pleasure and urging her on.

"Fly for me, Molly," he growled against her ear.

She scratched his back, trying to hold on, to make the magic of the long-awaited moment last. In the end she couldn't do it. The orgasm ripped through her, overwhelming her body, her mind, her heart. Her pussy contracted in endless waves of satisfaction. She gasped, the world a swirling vortex, and clung to him in the wonder of it. After all that twisting and stretching in his hands, she flew and flew and flew.

THE SEVENTH DAY

She woke the next morning exhausted and satisfied, still tangled in his arms. His head was thrown back in sleep, his scruffy dreadlocks strewn across his pillow. She was curled up against his shoulder. A small stretch awakened aching muscles, and blush-inducing memories. When she stirred, he stirred too, running a hand across her stomach and beneath her hip. A moment later, after fumbling with necessities, he was pressing inside her yet another time.

Half awake, the sensations were softened, edged with the cushioning of dreams. Was she dreaming this now? Had she dreamed the numerous times he'd taken her throughout the night? Had she dreamed the endless parade of shuddering orgasms he'd coaxed from her?

He turned and pressed her down to the bed with the force of his penetration, then lifted her, limp and pliable, to mount him in his lap. She climbed him, using his shoulders for leverage. He nipped her just below the ear, yanking her hips back down each time she pushed up from his thighs.

No, not dreaming.

He grabbed her face, kissing her hard, thrusting his tongue as deep as his cock was inside her. She moaned, letting him rock her on his shaft with strong, demanding hands. *Take me. Use me.* He grabbed a fistful of her curls and pulled her head back, baring her neck for his bite. She pressed against the solid heat of him, wanting him closer, ever closer. Wanting to disappear inside of him.

With a grunt, he pressed her back down onto the bed again, kneeling between her thighs and yanking her legs up over his shoulders. He grabbed her breasts painfully and then held her down, one palm pressed firmly just below her windpipe. If he wanted to, he could steal her air—the look he gave her told her he knew it. Instead he leaned down to kiss her again. She bit him, a wild sleepy creature who wasn't civilized just yet. He chuckled and grabbed her hands, pinning her arms over her head.

She squirmed beneath him—for his amusement only, since she knew he would release her when it pleased him, and not a moment before. But she didn't want to be released. His hands clinched tighter, his body pressing her down. His forceful thighs parted hers wider and he slid inside her in a maddening rhythm that stoked her g-spot to life with mind-melting pleasure. She stretched and arched for him. When he growled for her to come, she fought him and kicked her legs, hopelessly spread and conquered. With a sudden, shimmering cohesion of sensation, she reached a wrenching peak. As her pussy milked his cock in rhythmic spasms, he pressed against her, twisting a fist in her hair. She gasped at the pain, but her orgasm floated on before dissipating into an all-over weight of satiety. She relaxed beneath him, reveling in each sensation: the emptying of her pussy when he pulled out, the slide of his skin as he leaned away. Then he was back, gathering her up and pressing his rough cheek against her forehead.

Slowly, like a flower unfolding, her mind expanded into alert awareness. *Your Master comes today.* It would only be hours now until she saw him again. Mephisto was watching her, reading her face again with that strange facility of his.

"Today's the day."

His voice was kept carefully equivocal. Not happy, or disappointed. Not enthusiastic or angry. Just...blank. She could feel him pulling away from her emotionally, feel the separation as if it were a tangible thing. The loss of something he'd given her, and now chose to reclaim.

Mephisto was no one's, and no one ever belonged to him.

"Show me your arm," he said quietly.

Molly was relieved to have a mundane task to do in the moment. She still felt singed by the passion of the morning's encounter—one she somehow sensed had been their last. He carefully unwrapped the gauze bandage with the same fingers he'd pressed to her windpipe. The burn was shiny and red, but no longer swollen. Molly thought perhaps it wouldn't even leave a scar, at least not a raised one.

"It looks better," he said.

"Yes, Master."

"It's possible I over-reacted yesterday."

She giggled softly. "I'm so clumsy sometimes. My Master knows it. He'll just shake his head when he sees this."

"Yes. He didn't sound too surprised yesterday on the phone. He was actually shocked that you hadn't managed to get yourself into more trouble."

She lowered her eyes. "Did you tell him about...everything, Master?"

"No, but I will. The good and the bad. He might as well know the things you were punished for, as well as the things you handled well."

She wondered if he would tell Master about last night, when he had called her Molly, and made love to her. Repeatedly. Instead she asked, "Are you really going to give him the harness?"

"Yes. But now you're asking too many questions. You can ask me one more thing about our time together. Anything. But only one more thing, so choose carefully."

Perhaps he thought it would take her a while to narrow it down to one question, but it didn't. "Why did you take me out to the park yesterday? To that creek?"

He was silent a long while. "I just wanted to see you there. I had my own questions."

She wanted to ask if his questions had been answered, but her stingy quota of questions was already up. Her gaze fell on the cage. She had expected to sleep there last night, but now she realized her cage-time was over for the time being. Unless Master became interested in caging her, but that didn't seem very likely.

"Will you miss the cage?" he asked.

Damn. How did he *do* that?

"I... I think I will miss it a little, Master. It was a nice place to feel safe. To feel under your control."

"You can spend some time in there after breakfast. I don't need you for anything." He was tracing agile fingers over her breasts, bringing her nipples to a peak. She sighed, feeling the familiar throb of desire stoked to life again. Alone in the cage...bored...nothing to think about but...

"Master... Am I still... May I...?"

"Don't even think about it," he laughed. "Greedy girl. Yes, our time is almost up and the rules are relaxing a little. But I think you've had plenty of orgasms for the moment. If anything, I need to get you more worked up for your reunion with your Master. It's the least I can do for him, after he was kind enough to share you with me."

Later, after breakfast, she realized she would have done better to keep her mouth shut. He clamped her nipples and put the harness on her, with stinging oiled-up shafts in her ass and pussy. She was already hopelessly horny before she even crawled into the cage. An hour later he took off the clamps and loosened the harness just enough to slip a remote-controlled vibrator down inside it. By the time he released her just before dinner, she'd had more than enough of the cage.

* * * * *

At dinner, Mephisto added another chair to the table. Molly stared at it from her knees. He cocked his head, looking at her like she was an idiot.

"I know you know how to use a chair. Sit."

He unpacked takeout food, salads and sandwiches, as Molly sat wringing her hands in her lap. She felt she ought to either be helping, or else on her knees. He ignored her discomfort, serving her and even asking what she wanted to drink. He gave her her own glass and her own set of silverware—the first time in a weeks' time she'd eaten anything not from his hands. The thought depressed her a little, but she understood his intentions. This was a transition period, a decompression phase between Masters. *You'll be returned to your Master soon.*

It unsettled her that she wasn't nearly as impatient as she expected to be. Certainly she was excited to see her Master, but on the second day she'd thought she would have almost expired with craving by this point. Somehow, Mephisto had captured her. Now, he was letting her go. She ate at his side as he wished, but she still kept a respectable silence. It was strange to feed herself.

She missed the taste of his fingers.

She heard a small sob and realized it had come from her. Her throat closed up so she couldn't swallow, and her eyes filled with tears. She kept eating, small bites so she didn't choke, and he watched her a while before he put his hand on her hand.

"It's okay to cry. But I'd like you to tell me the reason."

She looked up at him, blinking through tears. "I think it's mostly...that I'm going to miss you."

"I'll miss you too," he said calmly, as if she wasn't going into full breakdown mode beside him. "I enjoyed our time together."

"Me, too," she said, latching onto his cordial tone like a life raft. "I enjoyed serving you, Master."

"Are you happy?"

His question came too quickly, too unexpectedly. She wasn't prepared for it. "What do you mean?" she stalled. "Happy to see my Master?"

"I mean," he said, a touch impatiently, "are you happy? Are you content in your life with him?"

She was silent a long moment. "Why are you asking me this?"

"Because he asked me to. And because I hope you would confide in me if you weren't happy."

"I am happy. Very happy!"

"He would love you either way, you know. He told me to tell you that too."

Molly stared at Mephisto, trying to untangle this new, brutal conversation. Her heart seized in her chest. "Does he not... Does he not want...?" She couldn't finish the words.

Mephisto looked at her with bemused affection. "Don't worry, kitten. It's *your* happiness he's worried about. As you know, he does what he wants in life, and his needs are well met by a very talented companion." He took one of her curls and pulled it in a soft tease. "He wants to be sure you're happy too, and he doesn't completely trust you to tell him the truth when you're in role. Not that a well-trained slave like you would lie..."

She bit her lip, flushing.

"It's only," he said, brushing back her hair, "that slaves sometimes feel they must tell Master what he wants to hear."

His tone, his soft touching of her hair was meant to reassure, but she was shaking with anxiety. "You're telling me the truth? He's not making plans to let me go, to release me? If you know—please—you have to tell me—"

"Release you? I never said anything about him wanting to release you. He's never indicated anything like that to me. In fact, I don't think there's any other owner of my acquaintance who cares so deeply about his slave. Just calm down, Molly."

He took a sip of water and leaned back in his chair, while Molly tried to still the galloping pace of her heart. She wanted the cage. The harness. The snake whip and a year of orgasm denial. Anything but this horrible conversation.

"You know, I did this to you," he said. "I made you who you are."

"That's not true." Her slave face fell away, replaced by indignation. "I was always meant to be this way. You're not God. You didn't make me any way—"

"Okay." Again, he put his hand over hers. "Breathe, Molly. And you're right. I didn't make you into a slave, but I had a lot to do with introducing you to Clayton. I set you on this path. To be honest, I was surprised where it ended up."

"Surprised how?" asked Molly slowly.

"Surprised at how much you gave up for him." He looked uncomfortable, a novelty that unsettled her even further. Then the look was gone. "Are you happy, Molly?"

She swallowed, wiping away the last of her tears. "Yes." She pursed her lips. "Yes, Mephisto, I'm happy."

A full minute or more went by before he spoke again. "Slavery fits you like a glove, kitten. So it doesn't surprise me. But look in my eyes and promise me that if you ever need help, you'll come to me. If you're ever unhappy. If the fit starts to slip."

"I promise," she said. She looked into dark eyes that were lighter than she'd thought. It was so hard to really see them in the somber light of the dark club where he lived.

"Good enough," he said. He looked at his watch. "It's almost time for Club Mephisto to open. Go get cleaned up and lie down under my desk until your Master arrives to take you home."

* * * * *

She cried a little more curled up under Mephisto's big table. Perhaps in an effort to distract and refocus her, or perhaps in some quest for symmetry, he sat down in the midst of the club's busy opening preparations and pulled her face into his lap under the table once more. He unzipped and handed down the flavored condom. Now, she was much more adept at handling the slick barrier. Before she'd even unrolled it fully, she was moving her tongue across the smooth, bulbous head of his cock. She let herself love him in the moment. She only really loved Master, but for a short while, this man had been her Master too. He'd trained her and challenged her. He'd revealed truths to her and made it so she couldn't look away. He'd offered her a protection that wouldn't end when he handed her leash back to her Master. Somehow she sensed it was a protection that had been there all along.

Maybe he once again perceived her thoughts as she sucked and caressed him. Even hidden away under the table, she sensed he was feeling the same heightened emotion she felt. When he finally came, his broad cock pulsing in her throat, he spread both hands on either side of her face and left them there. There seemed some power in his touch, some branding. He held her head like that for long moments before he pulled away. He reached down then to clip on her silver leash, and she curled up at his feet. Waiting.

Waiting, such a familiar feeling. It was still a couple more hours after that before Master arrived. By that time, she was anxious. She was jumping out of her skin to see him. When Mephisto tugged her leash, she crawled out and knelt up, head bowed, her hands folded in her lap and her thighs slightly parted the way he liked. Tears of joy spilled over when her Master lifted her chin to greet her, and an ecstatic smile lit her face. Then she was crying, really crying, and Master was pulling her up by her leash and hugging her close, licking the tears right off her face.

HOME

Master took her home, stripped her coat off, and led her straight to the bedroom. She gazed at him from her knees as he undressed. His hands were rough and possessive as he lifted her, and Molly nearly began sobbing with relief when he bent her over the footboard. He drove into her, skin-to-skin, no distancing barrier between them. He ran his fingers all over her, whispering about how much he'd missed her, how much time they had to make up. He fucked her with a delicious, vigorous intensity that had her sinking right back down into her place as his adoring toy.

Afterward he went back out to the living room to sort through the mail Mrs. Jernigan had laid aside while he was away. Molly knelt at his feet, feeling utterly relaxed and content to be home again attending to him in ways she was used to. But when he finished the mail, he picked up the black bag of Mephisto's and investigated the contents with a smile.

"I take it you had an interesting stay with him. He and I are meeting for lunch next week, and he promises to tell me all about your adventures. A chastity harness," he murmured, with a look that set her blushing. "Didn't I tell you he wouldn't be as free with your orgasms?"

"Master, he was a terror."

He threw back his head and laughed. She loved when she managed to amuse him, but in this case it had come at a very high price to her tortured libido.

"Ah, you sweet thing. I would have enjoyed seeing you suffer under his dominion." So her Master had known exactly what she was going to be subjected to. She gave him a teasing, slightly miffed look from under her lashes. That amused him even more, and he stroked her cheek affectionately. "My little treasure. You see, you are as lucky to have me as I am to have you."

"I *am* lucky, Master. I never forget it," she said with meaning. He sobered and gazed down at her.

"Do you not ever worry, little one, about what provisions I've made for you should I become...unable to fulfill my obligations as your Master?"

"Oh." One short syllable, but her voice trembled. "Well...I... I don't like to think about that."

"I will grow old well before you. And you never know. I could die in a car crash tomorrow."

"I want to be with you forever, Master," she said. "And if you... If something happens to you..."

"You'll what? Go and fling yourself from a cliff? Since I won't be able to give instructions from beyond the grave, let me be explicit with you now. No cliffs."

He was smiling again. Molly flushed a little, amazed that he could discuss such a painful subject so casually. "Master, I hope I die before you."

"And I hope you don't. With that in mind, I might as well tell you there are arrangements in place. A nice allowance to keep you comfortable for the remainder of your lifetime, and someone to take over for me. Should it come to that," he added. "And don't look so traumatized. It's someone you know very well."

"Master Mephisto," Molly said softly. It was all suddenly clear. Mephisto's talk, and her intense sojourn with him.

"Yes," her Master confirmed. "In the event I can't care for you, you'll go to him."

Her gaze shot to his in surprised disbelief. "You are... You are going to *bequeath* me to Master Mephisto? Is that even legal?"

She shut her mouth, her face flaming red. To burst out at him in that disrespectful tone... She bowed her head in the face of his silent displeasure. "I am so sorry, Master."

"I understand this discussion has you on edge. But of course, you'll be whipped for that."

"Yes, Master. I should be."

"It is not your decision, but mine," he snapped, all humor fled.

She bowed and pressed her lips to his fine leather shoes, carefully, so as not to smudge them with lipstick, then rested her forehead on the floor.

"Please, Master," she sighed against the carpet. Her shoulders shook with emotion. Tonight of all nights, she couldn't bear his anger. She stayed still for long moments, and tried not to cry and further anger him. After a couple tense minutes, he took her hair hard in his hands and pulled her head up. She gazed at him, ignoring the burn in her scalp, relieved to see patience and indulgence in his eyes.

"Now. Will you let me finish?"

"Yes, Master," she said in her most abject whisper.

"I was going to tell you that Master Mephisto agreed to help you seek a new Master in the event I predecease you or become too infirm to handle you as you're accustomed. I asked him to do me the honor some time ago. He's very intelligent and possesses great integrity. He takes good measure of people and knows the quality Masters in the community. If you'll remember, it was Mephisto who put you in my way not so many years ago, when you were a young, curious submissive."

She blinked, digesting this information. It was true that Mephisto had his fingers on the very pulse of the thriving local BDSM community, and that he understood her deeply, especially after all they'd shared the past week. For just a moment she lifted her hands from their designated position in her lap to touch her heart.

"Master, your forethought and care is so appreciated. I love you so much."

He stroked her hair gently. "There now. My well-mannered slave is back. And so you see, there was a greater reason for your week with Master Mephisto. The better he knows you, your ins and outs, the better he can assist you in the unfortunate event of my demise."

A horrible, soul-rending thought occurred to her then. She drew in a heavy breath, her eyes wide in sudden alarm.

"Master—you are not sick—are you? Your trip—"

He smiled and shook his head. "I didn't lie to you about my trip, girl. It was just business. And do I look sick to you? I'm not leaving this life anytime soon, I hope. But if I did, would you trust Mephisto to help select another Master for you?" He did not ask "If you wished it," because he knew she would wish for another Master, *need* another Master to truly live happily. She considered a moment, thought back over their weekend together, and Mephisto's strange, candid questioning the last day.

"I—yes—I suppose I would trust him, Master."

"And remember, he is only to assist you. It will be your choice, of course. The initial choice is always yours, and the decision to cede more and more power is, ultimately, also your choice. We spoke about this in the beginning of our relationship, you remember."

"Yes, Master." She did remember their long talks and negotiations. Promises were made on both sides.

Her Master regarded her thoughtfully. "Perhaps he might make an offer to you himself. Would you like to belong to Mephisto?"

Tears gathered behind her eyes. "I don't want to belong to anyone but you, Master. Please don't make me think of these things. I'm growing upset, I can't help it. Oh—Master—"

The tears flowed, the floodgates breached. He reached for her and pulled her into his lap. She sobbed quietly in his arms, soaking his silk shirt, listening to his heart beat against her ear. He stroked her hair and held her, massaging her back until the small storm passed. She raised her head, wrung out and ashamed.

"I'm sorry for losing control, Master. Thank you for soothing me. I'm so sorry."

"It's been a difficult week for you, I know, my pet. And there's no need to worry about these things right now. Of course the idea of a new Master is distressing to you. But you are mine as much as any of the other valuables I own, and I refuse to leave you unprotected should the worst occur."

"Thank you, Master," she said. "You are so kind to me. I love you."

"I love you too." He shifted, putting her back on the floor beside him. "You know, if you were to go to him, he would be a fine owner. He's a good, conscientious man. Don't you agree?"

"Yes, Master." She looked up at him, asking permission to speak openly, which he granted with a subtle nod. "It's only that he scares me a little. Actually, a lot. I think he would be a difficult Master to serve."

"Ah, well." He made a dismissive gesture with one well-manicured hand. "I'm not precisely easy. You were scared with me too at first. You were terrified. Don't you remember?"

She looked sheepish. It was true. There were many months in the beginning that she had struggled and shaken with confusion and fear, and now, just a few years later, she was so happy and content in her service.

"It's true, Master. You know what's best for me. Please forgive me for these silly fears and my outburst. I'm better now."

He patted her head with a sigh. "That's a good girl. Now go and get the whip."

"Yes, Master."

She crawled to get it from behind the ottoman near the fireplace, and returned to him with the whip in her mouth. He took it from her and ran a gentle hand down the side of her damp cheek.

She kissed his fingers and turned with a sigh, lowering herself into position, her hands in fists beside her head, her ass high in the air.

The End

Be sure to read the economy-priced companion novella, *Molly's Lips: Club Mephisto Retold,* to hear this same story from Mephisto's point of view.

Club Mephisto is also available in audio, read by Tess Irondale, beginning in February of 2016.

BURN FOR YOU
THE CONCLUSION TO THE CLUB MEPHISTO STORIES

When Molly loses her longtime Master, she feels lost, angry. Confused. She's unsure of her future, even her calling to the BDSM lifestyle. She knows her Master always intended her to go to his friend Mephisto next, but their emotionally—and sexually—fraught history is still a confusion of desire and fear in her mind.

Mephisto wants to help Molly, but he doesn't want to force her into service she's not sure she wants. He owes it to Clayton to help her find happiness, but how? Molly and Mephisto advance and retreat from one another as they try to untangle their complex feelings. More and more it seems their tense standoff will only end one way…

AN EXCERPT FROM BURN FOR YOU

"Master Mephisto?"

Mephisto turned at the sharp voice of his dungeon assistant, Glenn. "What is it?"

"A woman by the door. I think she's altered."

"If she's altered, she can't come in. You know the rules."

"I think it's Molly."

Mephisto spun toward the door. Glenn was right. It was Molly, but she barely looked like herself. Dirty, disheveled, her face and eyes swollen, probably from substance abuse. She yanked at her collar, screaming something he couldn't hear across the room. Then her eyes met his and she came storming his way, shrugging off the doorman trying to restrain her. She barreled right through a whip scene, evading injury by dumb luck.

"What the fuck is wrong with you?" he yelled, grabbing her arm. "He could have taken your eye out."

"Get it off me," she screamed, yanking at her neck, at the slim collar still gleaming there. "Take it off me, God damn it. I know you know how."

The dungeon monitors were drifting closer in case they had to help, and patrons were starting to watch. Molly yanked at her collar like a full-blown maniac. She was on something, rabid, out of her mind. He dragged her back past the bar into his private rooms. He flipped on the light in the kitchen and looked down at the girl in his grasp. Her eyes were dilated, her skin pallid. She'd lost ten pounds at least since he saw her last. Six weeks ago?

"What are you on?" It came out a growl. Mephisto didn't allow drugs in his club and he didn't allow them in his life. "What the fuck have you been doing with yourself?"

She ignored him, pulling so hard on the collar he worried she'd injure her neck. She let out an ear rending scream. "Take it off! Get it off me!"

"Okay, I'll take it off. When you calm down, I'll take it off. Let go of it."

He took her hands, restraining her with some effort. There were garish bruises around her neck. Who knew how long she'd been trying to get it off? But pulling it right through her neck wasn't the way to do it. Her small hands struggled in his.

"Let go of me," she moaned. "Let go!"

"I'll let go when you stop fighting me. Don't touch it. I need a special tool to get it off but I won't go get it until you calm down."

She sucked in air. Some shred of awareness flickered in her eyes. Her gaze darted around his kitchen and she licked dry lips. He'd lay odds she was on some hallucinogen. Not unknown for the old Molly. "Sit down," he said slowly and clearly. "Sit down and I'll take your collar off."

He led her to a chair at the table and she sank down. She shook all over, so hard he could practically hear it. She was in her usual pre-Clayton gear. Short skirt, nearly non-existent top. It was thirty degrees outside. He got a blanket from the bedroom and draped it around her. She reached again for the metal band around her neck, arrested by his disapproving sound. Glenn peeked in the door.

"Everything okay?"

"She'll be fine. Watch her a minute."

Mephisto stalked to the club's storage room, rooted through hardware and drawers of tools until he found the micro-screwdriver he needed. Molly wouldn't be the first slave he'd sprung from a "permanent" collar, nor would she be the last. He returned to the kitchen to find Molly glaring at Glenn with a murderous look.

"She's not quite herself, is she? You want me to call anyone?" Glenn asked.

"The loony bin?" Mephisto suggested. "Not for her. For me. No. She'll be fine, but I might not be back out there tonight."

"We'll hold down the fort."

Glenn left and Mephisto approached the sickly, shivering girl at his table. She seemed to be coming down already, her energy flagging. God knew how she'd gotten here in her condition. He could picture her wandering down the streets of downtown Seattle, clawing at her collar and screaming like a psycho. He was suddenly bone-chillingly relieved she'd found her way here.

"Let me see." He reached for the shining eternity collar, pushing her knotted, lank hair to the side. Her hair used to be her crowning glory, glossy and beautiful, but now it was dull, unwashed. She was trying to sit still but random shudders seized her small frame. "What are you on?" Mephisto asked again, now that she seemed slightly more lucid. "Are you going to go into heart failure on me? What did you take?"

"I don't know. I got it from someone."

"Who?"

She shrugged. "I don't know."

"Okay." He sighed. "Where were you?"

"Somewhere. I don't remember."

"At home? At a restaurant? At a club?"

"A club. Somewhere."

Somewhere on Pike Street, no doubt. Mephisto scrubbed a hand over his face. He had to get her collar off before she started clawing at it again. He traced around the smooth edges until he found the tiny depression he was looking for. "Be very still," he said. And then, "Are you sure?"

"Take it off." Her voice was firm. "I'm not his slave anymore."

Fair enough. He lined up the tiny screwdriver with the delicate, almost invisible release. She wasn't the only one shaking. His hands suddenly felt too big, too clumsy for this moment. He poked the sharp tool into the clasp until he managed to wiggle it loose. The collar opened and he eased it from her ravaged neck.

She turned to him. She was breathing hard, her chest rising and falling. "Give it to me."

"No." Not a chance. She'd calmed somewhat, but she was still out of her mind.

"Give it to me!"

"The screaming won't work. You're not getting it until you're down. Here are your choices. Go to the hospital. Go to jail. Spend the night here."

She stood and moved toward the door. "I'm leaving. I'm going home."

He stepped in front of her with a grim look. "I'll repeat your choices one more time. Hospital. Jail. Here."

"You can't keep me here! You don't control me."

"It appears no one controls you. Even you."

"You can't make me stay here against my will. That's kidnapping."

"Okay. Jail then. Hospital will cost too much." Mephisto got out his phone.

"Give me that collar!" She launched herself at him but he held the collar over his head, subduing her with one tight arm around her waist. She flailed, spitting at him. "You're an asshole!"

"Yes, and an abuser. I remember."

"And a criminal!"

"Says the girl who's high on some illegal substance." He pulled her over to the sink and made her drink an entire glass of water, even though most of it ended up on his clothes, and then took her to the bathroom. "Sit down and piss," he said. "And if you dare go anywhere but in the bowl I'll fucking destroy your ass."

She scowled and used the toilet, then stood and defiantly kicked off her thong panties and wisp of a skirt. "Are you going to rape me now?"

"There is nothing on earth I'd find less appealing at this moment. Put your skirt back on."

"Fuck you."

With a sigh, Mephisto picked up her skirt and panties and dragged them, along with the resisting woman, into his room. He flung her discarded clothes into a cage in the corner. Then he turned to Molly. "In you go."

"Fuck you!"

"One more time, because I know you're high and stupid right now. Hospital. Jail. Here. Pick your fucking choice."

She kicked him hard in the shin, which fucking hurt, then drew her knee back to aim for his balls. Before she could complete such an ill-advised attack, he picked her up and tossed her into the rectangular cage, shutting the door and locking it while she pounded on the bars. "You're going to be in so much fucking trouble when I call the police," she screeched. "This is kidnapping!"

"This is tough love. I'll let you out when whatever is in your system has worn off."

"I hate you. I hate you!" Bang, bang, bang on the bars. He sat on the edge of the bed and watched to be sure she wouldn't hurt herself. She banged for a minute, two minutes, but then she went still and lay back, and the sobbing started. Wails and sobs and threats of what would happen to him. "I have money, you asshole!" she shrieked. "I'm fucking rich, and you're toast!"

Mephisto wondered how much of Clayton's fortune Molly had managed to lose or burn through in the last month and a half. Not too much, he hoped. He shouldn't have left her alone, even though she sent him away. He realized that now.

"I hate you. I hate you. *I hate you.*" Screams turned to whines and whines turned to whimpers and then she was all raged out and there was only her vicious glare. He studied the slim metal circlet between his fingers, remembering better times. She followed him with her eyes as he stood and crossed the room to lay her collar on top of his chest of drawers. Such a beautiful, delicate work of art. He remembered when Clayton had first showed it to him. He'd had it specially made for her.

"It would have killed him to see you this way," Mephisto said. Not to her, because she was in no state to listen. He just said it because it was the dismal truth.

Burn for You is available wherever ebooks are sold.

Other intensely emotional BDSM series
by Annabel Joseph

The Rough Love series

There's rough sex, and then there's rough love. The challenge is learning the difference between them...

Chere's a high class call girl trapped in a self-destructive spiral, and "W" is the mysterious and sexually voracious client who refuses to tell her his name. Over the span of four years, their tortured relationship unwinds by fits and starts, encompassing fear and loneliness, mistrust, aggression, literal and figurative bondage, and moments of excruciating pain.

But there's also caring and longing, and heartfelt poetry. There are two deeply damaged people straining to connect despite the daunting emotional risks. When he slaps her face or grasps her neck, it's not to hurt, but to hold. His rough passions are a plea, and Chere's the only one so far who's been able to understand...

The Rough Love series is:
#1 *Torment Me*
#2 *Taunt Me*
#3 *Trust Me*

The Cirque Masters series

Enter a world where performers' jaw-dropping strength, talent, and creativity is matched only by the decadence of their kinky desires. Cirque du Monde is famous for mounting glittering circus productions, but after the Big Top goes dark, you can find its denizens at *Le Citadel*, a fetish club owned by Cirque CEO Michel Lemaitre—where anything goes. This secret world is ruled by dominance and submission, risk and emotion, and a fearless dedication to carnal pleasure in all its forms. Love in the circus can be as perilous as aerial silks or trapeze, and secrets run deep in this intimate society. Run away to the circus, and soar with the Cirque Masters—a delight for the senses, and for the heart.

The Cirque Masters series is:
#1 *Cirque de Minuit* (Theo's story)
#2 *Bound in Blue* (Jason's story)
#3 *Master's Flame* (Lemaitre's story)

The Comfort series

Have you ever wondered what goes on in the bedrooms of Hollywood's biggest heartthrobs? In the case of Jeremy Gray, the reality is far more depraved than anyone realizes. Brutal desires, shocking secrets, and a D/s relationship (with a hired submissive "girlfriend") that's based on a contract rather than love. It's just the beginning of a four-book saga following Jeremy and his Hollywood friends as they seek comfort in fake, manufactured relationships. Born of necessity—and public relations—these attachments come to feel more and more real. What does it take to live day-to-day with an A-list celebrity? Patience, fortitude, and a whole lot of heart. Oh, and a *very* good pain tolerance for kinky mayhem.

The Comfort series is:
#1 *Comfort Object* (Jeremy's story)
#2 *Caressa's Knees* (Kyle's story)
#3 *Odalisque* (Kai's story)
#4 *Command Performance* (Mason's story)

A Q & A WITH ANNABEL JOSEPH
ABOUT THE MEPHISTO SERIES, BDSM AND LOVE, AND OTHER COMPLICATED THINGS...

Q. Of all the books you've written, the Mephisto series seems to be the most polarizing. Can you tell us a little about how this series came to be?

A. The Mephisto books were actually my first foray into a harder Master/slave, total power exchange dynamic. I was pretty deep in the lifestyle at that time, first of all. I was also reading super hardcore books like Molly Weatherfield's Carrie books and Anneke Jacob's *As She's Told*. I also became friends with a man on Fetlife (aka Facebook for kinky people) who probably wouldn't self-identify as a Master, but he became the main model for the character who would eventually become Mephisto. He had dreadlocks and everything. So I started writing...

Q. What do you mean, he became the "main model"?

A. I drew from a lot of sources to put together *Club Mephisto*, but this friend was the inspiration for the actual man, like, physically and psychically. As I read this person's posts, I came to see he was very intelligent, very safety oriented, and very, very, *very* kinky and hardcore, which can sometimes seem at odds with the whole safety thing, but not in his case. I mean, he was super hardcore and really scary, but safety was always foremost in his mind, and that fascinated me (and I guess comforted me as I read his hair-raising posts.)

Q. Does he really own a club, like the character in your book?

A. He doesn't own a club in real life, but he's a notable member of the kink community where he lives. I imagine his house sometimes transforms into an impromptu Club Mephisto. He gives themed parties and so on.

Q. Sounds fun!

A. I know, right!! But this dude has no idea he inspired a whole series. I didn't want to tell him. I was too shy and embarrassed.

Q. That was going to be my next question, whether he knew he was "Master Mephisto," and if you consulted with him to write *Molly's Lips*, since it was written from the Master's point of view.

A. No, there were no consultations. I never actually got to meet him face to face, although we tried once, when I was in his city for a conference. I was only there a couple days though, and it didn't pan out.

But it wasn't hard to write Mephisto's point of view, because the whole time I was writing Molly's point of view, I knew what Mephisto was thinking and feeling. I didn't write *Molly's Lips* for a long time, because I didn't think anyone would be interested in reading the same story twice, but some of my readers kept urging me to do it (looking at you, Ingrid) and in the end I was glad they did, because it wasn't the same story at all. From his perspective, with his motivations and thoughts, it was a whole new book. There were a lot of activities we didn't get to see when we were stuck in Molly's perspective—his confrontation with Jamie when they went back into the bedroom, his trip to visit Lorna at the fetish shop, and of course the things he was thinking about Molly as he was putting her through her paces.

Q. And the conversations he had with her Master. It was fun to eavesdrop on those.

A. Yes, those were really great to write, because I got to show more of Clayton too. Molly has such a hemmed-in world view. It's by her choice, but still. She sees and hears very little aside from her Master's voice and signals. I think that was a big part of her challenge in being at Mephisto's. He forced her to deal with things she hadn't had to deal with while she was living in her Master's velvet cage. Not just the orgasm denial, although that was a huge strategy of manipulation for Mephisto. It was things like doing dishes, ironing clothes, working at the club, going to the park and eating ice cream, and being confronted with the career she'd abandoned. He did all those things intentionally, as Molly suspected. Her stay there was planned and executed with a great depth of thought.

Q. That's pretty sexy.

A. It's sexy when someone cares enough to make complicated plans to dig inside your mind. Sexy and maybe a little creepy. But mostly sexy!

Q. You won't get any argument here. One of the most fascinating things about Molly is how she finds really painful and unpleasant things arousing. She's turned on by sacrifice and being forced to do things she doesn't like to do.

A. In other words, by being a slave, haha. My view of slavery isn't everyone's view of slavery, but for me, BDSM slavery is very much about effacing your needs and wants in order to serve someone else, who, hopefully, is worthy of all the things you give up in the course of that service. If the person isn't caring or worthy, then the whole sexiness of the thing breaks down.

Q. Then it becomes abusive.

A. It's a fine line. I think if a slave is unhappy and unfulfilled, and forced to do things that bring them no pleasure, then yeah, that's not slavery anymore. That's something dark and sad. Ideally, slavery isn't sad. It's fulfilling to both the top and the bottom in the situation.

Q. Earlier, I used the word "polarizing" to describe this book. The reviews are all over the map, lots of five stars, lots of one stars. How do you explain that?

A. I never try to explain reviews. They're the reader's opinion, and everyone's allowed to have an opinion. I have noticed that *Club Mephisto*—much more than any of my other books—is a love-it-or-hate-it kind of experience. I think in order to love it, you have to have a pretty deep understanding of the psychology of dominance and submission.

If you're a BDSM dilettante—and it's perfectly fine to be a dilettante—maybe you're drawn to lighter play, softer scenes, hugs and kisses and traditional romance, you know, the proverbial pink fuzzy handcuffs that don't really lock. There's nothing wrong with that, but someone who's at that level of understanding and comfort with BDSM isn't going to relate to a dynamic like Molly and Clayton's, or Molly and Mephisto's. It'll shock and confuse them. You can see that in some of the reviews.

But for someone who's delved deeper into the psychology of power exchange, they understand Molly's mindset and maybe even identify with her needs. They understand that Clayton isn't a manipulative abuser, and that Mephisto isn't a satanic jerk. The characters in this series all choose the lives they're living, and they're all happy in those lives.

People who're comfortable with that idea have a much easier time picking up the love story in the Mephisto books. They're able to see the care and romance, and those are my five star readers. Those are the ones who write to me and tell me how deeply the books resonated with them. The one star readers probably weren't my readers to begin with, but that's okay. It's best if they move on.

Q. Let's talk about *Burn For You*. It took a long time for you to write it.

A. It didn't take a long time to write it. It was just a long time between finishing *Club Mephisto* and starting to work on *Burn For You*. There was actually a long time between *Club Mephisto* and *Molly's Lips*, and then *Burn For You* came out right after *Molly's Lips*, because I wrote those two one after the other.

Q. Why did you do it that way? Why the delay?

A. It's obvious, isn't it? I was afraid of where the story had to go. I knew some sad things had to happen to move Molly on from Clayton, whether by breakup, or mutual agreement, or illness, or death. No matter what, it was going to be awful and I didn't want to go there. From the very beginning, before I sat down to write *Club Mephisto*, I knew Molly was going to end up with Mephisto, but it seemed so unfair to Clayton, who I really, really came to like.

But once I wrote *Molly's Lips*, and put down the conversations between Mephisto and Clayton, I knew I had to just write the fucking finale. I had to tell the story, because that was the story and it couldn't be changed.

There were a lot of tears. Fortunately, I had a lot of readers behind me saying, *please, please write it for us. Yes, it will be sad, but it'll be okay.* And it was okay, but it was really wrenching and difficult. I was moving on in my own kink/lifestyle journey at the time, and I felt a lot of the things Molly felt in *Burn For You*. It was really claustrophobic, writing parts of that book.

Q. Which parts? Is that too personal to ask?

A. Well, nothing specific took place in my real life. None of those books were strictly autobiographical. It was more the change between the dynamic she'd had with Clayton, and the one she had to work out with Mephisto. It was the doubting and the sense of loss, and the sense of disequilibrium that I related to, because in my life, everything had been static for so long, and then it was turned on its ear, weirdly because of the success in my developing career as an author. There were a lot of adjustments in my personal life and relationship.

But we all have those experiences, where our lives change suddenly and we have to work through what's happened, and perhaps feel the same rage and helplessness that Molly felt during her transition. I think a lot of people can relate, even if not in a kink-relationship way.

Q. Do you think Molly and Mephisto are still together today? Are they a "forever couple"?

A. Oh, for sure they are, because they're a perfect match. Mephisto is the thoughtful, careful one who can keep Molly safe and happy, because she has no sense of self-preservation—she wants to give everything for love. So they balance each other out. Clayton said something to Mephisto, I don't remember the exact words, but it was something like, "Can you imagine what might happen to her if she falls into the wrong hands?" Because Molly lives to love and serve, sometimes to her detriment. She could really be taken advantage of if she ended up with an asshole.

Q. Luckily Mephisto isn't an asshole.

A. I never write assholes for heroes! Even if they act like assholes sometimes, there's always love and courage underneath. They have to be good men under all the Dominant bluster and posturing, and the subs have to be strong, even if they're surrendering. I mean, Molly is strong. She goes after what she wants. She works hard for her happiness in a world that isn't always supportive of women who choose to surrender.

Q. In a world where it's not always safe to surrender.

A. Yes. But with Mephisto, she's safe, which Clayton realized. Clayton has a lot of haters, but I really admired him. I'd like to write a book about a Master who's similar to Clayton someday. Or maybe a prequel to *Club Mephisto* and *Molly's Lips*. I'll call it *Clayton and Molly: the Dating Years*.

Q. Yes! Write it!

A. No, I can't. It would be too wistful, because I know they don't last. But maybe I can write some other Dominant who's like Clayton, who's just a good, steady, protective guy. But then, that's not as exciting as writing someone scary and charismatic like Mephisto. Oh well, forget it. I still like Clayton. Next!

Q. Let's talk about the Master/slave dynamic, as opposed to a less exacting Dom/sub relationship.

A. Or even a Top/bottom relationship. I wrote a Top/bottom dynamic in *Fever Dream*. Rubio didn't want anything to do with all the lifestyle titles and protocols. He just wanted to be in charge, and he wanted Petra to surrender to his will.

Q. There are so many ways to do it.

A. Yes, and in my books I like to write all kinds of dynamics, from hardcore Master/slave, to hardcore Dom/sub, to softer Dom/sub, to Top/bottom, to spanking-only books that don't have any BDSM at all (but probably the most power exchange.)

I think I do that so I don't get stuck in a rut. Honestly, I find any dynamic between two compelling characters to be interesting. If they're working things out, if they're discovering things about themselves and the other person, I find it compelling and sexy. I just want it to be real. I want them to be invested in their dynamic, whatever it is. The fact that there are countless possibilities for BDSM dynamics means I can write foreverrrrr.

Q. What book do you think comes closest to the intense Master/slave dynamic that Molly and Mephisto have?

A. Weirdly, I would have to say Chere and "W" in the Rough Love series. They're not what you'd traditionally think of as Master/slave, but he demands crazy, crazy, *crazy* amounts of control, perhaps even more than Clayton or Mephisto by the time he has Chere under his thumb in the third book. And yet, unlike Clayton and Mephisto, he has a lot less self-knowledge and is a lot less at ease with the things he desires.

When I was writing the Rough Love series, I kept whispering to myself, *This is crazy. He's freaking crazy.* But at the same time, their dynamic is serious as shit to him, and to her. They get caught up in it to an alarming degree. But, unlike the characters in the Mephisto series, they aren't always in control.

Well, until the end. You know, I always redeem them in the end. I want people to walk away from my books with positive feelings, and I want them to believe that ten, fifteen, twenty years down the road, the characters will still be happy in their relationships, no matter how fucked up those relationships might seem to people looking in from the outside. That's the Annabel Joseph promise.

Q. Cool! We'll hold you to it. Thanks for speaking with us about the Mephisto series, and for being so candid in your responses. We'll be dreaming of a real-life Mephisto tonight...

ABOUT THE AUTHOR

Annabel Joseph is a multi-published BDSM romance author. She writes mainly contemporary romance, although she has been known to dabble in the medieval and Regency eras. She is known for writing emotionally intense BDSM storylines, and strives to create characters that seem real—even flawed—so readers are better able to relate to them. She also writes vanilla erotic romance under the name Molly Joseph.

You can learn more about Annabel's books and sign up for her newsletter at www.annabeljoseph.com. You can also like her Facebook page (www.facebook.com/annabeljosephnovels) or follow her on Twitter (@annabeljoseph).

Annabel loves to hear from her readers at
annabeljosephnovels@gmail.com.

31869068R00085

Made in the USA
San Bernardino, CA
21 March 2016